Douglas Adams created all the various and contradictory manifestations of *The Hitchhiker's Guide to the Galaxy*: radio, novels, TV, computer game, stage adaptations, comic book and bath towel. A major movie is currently in development hell and will almost certainly be released any decade now. He lectured and broadcast around the world and was a patron of the Dian Fossey Gorilla Fund and Save the Rhino International.

He was born in Cambridge, UK and lived with his wife and daughter in Santa Barbara, California, where he died suddenly on 11 May 2001.

For more information, visit *www.douglasadams.com*

If you are interested in the works of Douglas Adams, you may like to join ZZ9 Plural Z Alpha, the official Hitchhiker's Guide to the Galaxy Appreciation Society, founded in 1980. For details of this fan-run club visit www.zz9.org or send a SAE/IRC to:

ZZ9 Plural Z Alpha
4 The Sycamores, Hadfield
Derbyshire, SK13 2BS, UK

by the same author

The Hitchhiker series:

The Hitchhiker's Guide to the Galaxy
The Restaurant at the End of the Universe
Life, the Universe and Everything
So Long, and Thanks for all the Fish
Mostly Harmless

The Dirk Gently series:

Dirk Gently's Holistic Detective Agency
The Long Dark Tea-time of the Soul

With John Lloyd:

The Meaning of Liff
The Deeper Meaning of Liff

With Mark Carwardine:

Last Chance to See . . .

By Terry Jones, based on a story/
computer game by Douglas Adams:

Starship Titanic

DOUGLAS ADAMS

So Long, and Thanks for all the Fish

Pan Books

First published 1984 by Pan Books

This edition published 1985 by Pan Books
an imprint of Pan Macmillan Ltd
Pan Macmillan, 20 New Wharf Road, London N1 9RR
Basingstoke and Oxford
Associated companies throughout the world
www.panmacmillan.com

In association with William Heinemann Ltd

ISBN 0 330 28700 1

47 48

A CIP catalogue record for this book is available from the British Library.

Typeset by SetSystems Ltd, Saffron Walden, Essex
Printed and bound in Great Britain by
Mackays of Chatham plc, Chatham, Kent

for Jane

with thanks

to Rick and Heidi for the loan of their stable event

to Mogens and Andy and all at Huntsham Court
for a number of unstable events

and especially to Sonny Mehta for being
stable through all events.

[illegible]

[illegible] the [illegible] Hitchhiker's [illegible] the [illegible] of the [illegible] of the Galaxy [illegible] regarded [illegible]

[illegible]

[illegible]

This [illegible] a problem [illegible] the people [illegible] were [illegible] or [illegible] this [illegible] of these [illegible] small [illegible] which [illegible] the small [illegible] which [illegible]

And so the problem [illegible] of the people [illegible] and most of [illegible] even [illegible] digital watches.

[illegible] made [illegible] mistake [illegible] getting down [illegible] the first place. And some said that even the trees [illegible] been a bad move, and that [illegible] should ever have left the oceans.

And then, one Thursday, nearly two thousand years after one man had been nailed to a tree for saying how great it would be to be nice to people for a change, [illegible] her own [illegible] suddenly realized what it was that had been going wrong all this time, and she finally knew how the world could be made a good and happy place. This time [illegible]

[illegible]

Prologue

Far out in the uncharted backwaters of the unfashionable end of the Western Spiral Arm of the Galaxy lies a small unregarded yellow sun.

Orbiting this at a distance of roughly ninety-two million miles is an utterly insignificant little blue-green planet whose ape-descended life forms are so amazingly primitive that they still think digital watches are a pretty neat idea.

This planet has – or had – a problem, which was this: most of the people living on it were unhappy for pretty much of the time. Many solutions were suggested for this problem, but most of these were largely concerned with the movements of small green pieces of paper, which is odd because on the whole it wasn't the small green pieces of paper which were unhappy.

And so the problem remained; lots of the people were mean, and most of them were unhappy, even the ones with digital watches.

Many were increasingly of the opinion that they'd all made a big mistake in coming down from the trees in the first place. And some said that even the trees had been a bad move, and that no one should ever have left the oceans.

And then, one Thursday, nearly two thousand years after one man had been nailed to a tree for saying how great it would be to be nice to people for a change, a girl sitting on her own in a small café in Rickmansworth suddenly realized what it was that had been going wrong all this time, and she finally knew how the world could be made a good and happy place. This time it was right, it would work, and no one would have to get nailed to anything.

Sadly, however, before she could get to a phone to tell anyone about it, the Earth was unexpectedly demolished to make way for a new hyperspace bypass, and so the idea was lost, seemingly for ever.

This is her story.

1

That evening it was dark early, which was normal for the time of year. It was cold and windy, which was normal.

It started to rain, which was particularly normal.

A spacecraft landed, which was not.

There was nobody around to see it except for some spectacularly stupid quadrupeds who hadn't the faintest idea what to make of it, or whether they were meant to make anything of it, or eat it, or what. So they did what they did to everything which was to run away from it and try to hide under each other, which never worked.

It slipped down out of the clouds, seemingly balanced on a single beam of light.

From a distance you would scarcely have noticed it through the lightning and the storm clouds, but seen from close to it was strangely beautiful – a grey craft of elegantly sculpted form: quite small.

Of course, one never has the slightest notion what size or shape different species are going to turn out to be, but if you were to take the findings of the latest Mid-Galactic Census report as any kind of accurate guide to statistical averages you would probably guess that the craft would hold about six people, and you would be right.

You'd probably guessed that anyway. The Census report, like most such surveys, had cost an awful lot of money and didn't tell anybody anything they didn't already know – except that every single person in the Galaxy had 2.4 legs and owned a hyena. Since this was clearly not true the whole thing had eventually to be scrapped.

The craft slid quietly down through the rain, its dim operating lights wrapping it in tasteful rainbows. It hummed very quietly, a hum which became gradually louder and deeper as it approached the ground, and which at an altitude of six inches became a heavy throb.

At last it dropped and was quiet.

A hatchway opened. A short flight of steps unfolded itself.

A light appeared in the opening, a bright light streaming out into the wet night, and shadows moved within.

A tall figure appeared in the light, looked around, flinched, and hurried down the steps, carrying a large shopping bag under its arm.

It turned and gave a single abrupt wave back to the ship. Already the rain was streaming through its hair.

'Thank you,' he called out, 'thank you very . . .'

He was interrupted by a sharp crack of thunder. He glanced up apprehensively, and in response to a sudden thought quickly started to rummage through the large plastic shopping bag, which he now discovered had a hole in the bottom.

It had large characters printed on the side which read (to anyone who could decipher the Centaurian alphabet) DUTY FREE MEGA-MARKET, PORT BRASTA, ALPHA CENTAURI. BE LIKE THE TWENTY-SECOND ELEPHANT WITH HEATED VALUE IN SPACE – BARK!

'Hold on!' the figure called, waving at the ship.

The steps, which had started to fold themselves back through the hatchway, stopped, re-unfolded, and allowed him back in.

He emerged again a few seconds later carrying a battered and threadbare towel which he shoved into the bag.

He waved again, hoisted the bag under his arm, and started to run for the shelter of some trees as, behind him, the spacecraft had already begun its ascent.

Lightning flitted through the sky and made the figure pause for a moment, and then hurry onwards, revising his path to give the trees a wide berth. He moved swiftly across the ground, slipping here and there, hunching himself against the rain which was falling now with ever-increasing concentration, as if being pulled from the sky.

His feet sloshed through the mud. Thunder grumbled over the hills. He pointlessly wiped the rain off his face and stumbled on.

More lights.

Not lightning this time, but more diffused and dimmer lights which played slowly over the horizon and faded.

The figure paused again on seeing them, and then redoubled his steps, making directly towards the point on the horizon at which they had appeared.

And now the ground was becoming steeper, sloping upwards, and after another two or three hundred yards it led at last to an obstacle. The figure paused to examine the barrier and then dropped the bag he was carrying over it before climbing over himself.

Hardly had the figure touched the ground on the other side when there came sweeping out of the rain towards him a machine, lights streaming through the wall of water. The figure pressed back as the machine streaked towards him. It was a low bulbous shape, like a small whale surfing – sleek, grey and rounded and moving at terrifying speed.

The figure instinctively threw up his hands to protect himself, but was hit only by a sluice of water as the machine swept past and off into the night.

It was illuminated briefly by another flicker of lightning crossing the sky, which allowed the soaked figure by the roadside a split-second to read a small sign at the back of the machine before it disappeared.

To the figure's apparent incredulous astonishment the sign read, 'My other car is also a Porsche.'

2

Rob McKenna was a miserable bastard and he knew it because he'd had a lot of people point it out to him over the years and he saw no reason to disagree with them except the obvious one which was that he liked disagreeing with people, particularly people he disliked, which included, at the last count, everybody.

He heaved a sigh and shoved down a gear.

The hill was beginning to steepen and his lorry was heavy with Danish thermostatic radiator controls.

It wasn't that he was naturally predisposed to be so surly, at least he hoped not. It was just the rain which got him down, always the rain.

It was raining now, just for a change.

It was a particular type of rain that he particularly disliked, particularly when he was driving. He had a number for it. It was rain type 17.

He had read somewhere that the Eskimos had over two hundred different words for snow, without which their conversation would probably have got very monotonous. So they would distinguish between thin snow and thick snow, light snow and heavy snow, sludgy snow, brittle snow, snow that came in flurries, snow that came in drifts, snow that came in on the bottom of your neighbour's boots all over your nice clean igloo floor, the snows of winter, the snows of spring, the snows you remember from your childhood that were so much better than any of your modern snow, fine snow, feathery snow, hill snow, valley snow, snow that falls in the morning, snow that falls at night, snow that falls all of a sudden just when you were going out fishing, and snow that despite all your efforts to train them the huskies have pissed on.

Rob McKenna had two hundred and thirty-one different types of rain entered in his little book, and he didn't like any of them.

He shifted down another gear and the lorry heaved its revs up. It grumbled in a comfortable sort of way about all the Danish thermostatic radiator controls it was carrying.

Since he had left Denmark the previous afternoon, he had been through types 33 (light pricking drizzle which made the roads slippery), 39 (heavy spotting), 47 to 51 (vertical light drizzle through to sharply slanting light to moderate drizzle freshening), 87 and 88 (two finely distinguished varieties of vertical torrential downpour), 100 (post-downpour squalling, cold), all the seastorm types between 192 and 213 at once, 123, 124, 126, 127 (mild and intermediate cold gusting, regular and syncopated cab-drumming), 11 (breezy droplets) and now his least favourite of all, 17.

Rain type 17 was a dirty blatter battering against his windscreen so hard that it didn't make much odds whether he had his wipers on or off.

He tested this theory by turning them off briefly, but as it turned out the visibility did get quite a lot worse.

It just failed to get better again when he turned them back on.

In fact one of the wiper blades began to flap off.

Swish swish swish flop swish swish flop swish swish flop swish flop swish flop flop flap scrape.

He pounded his steering wheel, kicked the floor, thumped his cassette player till it suddenly started playing Barry Manilow, thumped it again till it stopped, and swore and swore and swore and swore and swore.

It was at the very moment that his fury was peaking that there loomed swimmingly in his headlights, hardly visible through the blatter, a figure by the roadside.

A poor bedraggled figure, strangely attired, wetter than an otter in a washing machine, and hitching.

'Poor miserable sod,' thought Rob McKenna to himself, realizing that here was somebody with a better right to feel hard done by than himself, 'must be chilled to the bone. Stupid to be out hitching on a filthy night like this. All you get is cold, wet, and lorries driving through puddles at you.'

He shook his head grimly, heaved another sigh, gave the wheel a turn and hit a large sheet of water square on.

'See what I mean?' he thought to himself as he ploughed swiftly through it. 'You get some right bastards on the road.'

Splattered in his rear mirror a couple of seconds later was the reflection of the hitchhiker, drenched by the roadside.

For a moment he felt good about this. A moment or two later he felt bad about feeling good about it. Then he felt good about feeling bad about feeling good about it and, satisfied, drove on into the night.

At least it made up for having been finally overtaken by that Porsche he had been diligently blocking for the last twenty miles.

And as he drove on, the rainclouds dragged down the sky after him, for, though he did not know it, Rob McKenna was a Rain God. All he knew was that his working days were miserable and he had a succession of lousy holidays. All the clouds knew was that they loved him and wanted to be near him, to cherish him, and to water him.

3

The next two lorries were not driven by Rain Gods, but they did exactly the same thing.

The figure trudged, or rather sloshed, onwards till the hill resumed and the treacherous sheet of water was left behind.

After a while the rain began to ease and the moon put in a brief appearance from behind the clouds.

A Renault drove by, and its driver made frantic and complex signals to the trudging figure to indicate that normally he would have been delighted to give the figure a lift, only he couldn't this time because he wasn't going in the direction that the figure wanted to go, whatever direction that might be, and he was sure the figure would understand. He concluded the signalling with a cheery thumbs-up sign, as if to say that he hoped the figure felt really fine about being cold and almost terminally wet, and he would catch him next time around.

The figure trudged on. A Fiat passed and did exactly the same as the Renault.

A Maxi passed on the other side of the road and flashed its lights at the slowly plodding figure, though whether this was meant to convey a 'Hello' or a 'Sorry we're going the other way' or a 'Hey look, there's someone in the rain, what a jerk' was entirely unclear. A green strip across the top of the windscreen indicated that whatever the message was, it came from Steve and Carola.

The storm had now definitely abated, and what thunder there was now grumbled over more distant hills, like a man saying 'And another thing . . .' twenty minutes after admitting he's lost the argument.

The air was clearer now, the night cold. Sound travelled rather well. The lost figure, shivering desperately, presently reached a junction, where a side road turned off to the left. Opposite the turning stood a signpost which the figure suddenly hurried to and studied with feverish curiosity, only twisting away from it as another car passed suddenly.

And another.

The first whisked by with complete disregard, the second flashed meaninglessly. A Ford Cortina passed and put on its brakes.

Lurching with surprise, the figure bundled his bag to his chest and hurried forward towards the car, but at the last moment the Cortina spun its wheels in the wet and careered off up the road rather amusingly.

The figure slowed to a stop and stood there, lost and dejected.

As it chanced, the following day the driver of the Cortina went into hospital to have his appendix out, only due to a rather amusing mix up the surgeon removed his leg in error, and before the appendectomy could be rescheduled, the appendicitis complicated into an entertainingly serious case of peritonitis and justice, in its way, was served.

The figure trudged on.

A Saab drew to a halt beside him.

Its window wound down and a friendly voice said, 'Have you come far?'

The figure turned towards it. He stopped and grasped the handle of the door.

* * *

The figure, the car and its door handle were all on a planet called the Earth, a world whose entire entry in *The Hitchhiker's Guide to the Galaxy* comprised the two words 'Mostly harmless'.

The man who wrote this entry was called Ford Prefect, and he was at this precise moment on a far from harmless world, sitting in a far from harmless bar, recklessly causing trouble.

4

Whether it was because he was drunk, ill or suicidally insane would not have been apparent to a casual observer, and indeed there were no casual observers in the Old Pink Dog Bar on the lower South Side of Han Dold City because it wasn't the sort of place you could afford to do things casually in if you wanted to stay alive. Any observers in the place would have been mean hawklike observers, heavily armed, with painful throbbings in their heads which caused them to do crazy things when they observed things they didn't like.

One of those nasty hushes had descended on the place, a sort of missile crisis sort of hush.

Even the evil-looking bird perched on a rod in the bar had stopped screeching out the names and addresses of local contract killers, which was a service it provided for free.

All eyes were on Ford Prefect. Some of them were on stalks.

The particular way in which he was choosing to dice recklessly with death today was by trying to pay for a drinks bill the size of a small defence budget with an American Express card, which was not acceptable anywhere in the known Universe.

'What are you worried about?' he asked in a cheery kind of voice. 'The expiration date? Have you guys never heard of Neo-Relativity out here? There's whole new areas of physics which can take care of this sort of thing. Time dilation effects, temporal relastatics . . .'

'We are not worried about the expiration date,' said the man to whom he addressed these remarks, who was a dangerous barman in a dangerous city. His voice was a low soft purr, like the low soft purr made by the opening of an ICBM silo. A hand like a side of meat tapped on the bar top, lightly denting it.

'Well, that's good then,' said Ford, packing his satchel and preparing to leave.

The tapping finger reached out and rested lightly on the shoulder of Ford Prefect. It prevented him from leaving.

Although the finger was attached to a slablike hand, and the hand was attached to a clublike forearm, the forearm wasn't attached to anything at all, except in the metaphorical sense that it was attached by a fierce doglike loyalty to the bar which was its home. It had previously been more conventionally attached to the original owner of the bar, who on his deathbed had unexpectedly bequeathed it to medical science. Medical science had decided they didn't like the look of it and had bequeathed it right back to the Old Pink Dog Bar.

The new barman didn't believe in the supernatural or poltergeists or anything kooky like that, he just knew a useful ally when he saw one. The hand sat on the bar. It took orders, it served drinks, it dealt murderously with people who behaved as if they wanted to be murdered. Ford Prefect sat still.

'We are not worried about the expiration date,' repeated the barman, satisfied that he now had Ford Prefect's full attention. 'We are worried about the entire piece of plastic.'

'What?' said Ford. He seemed a little taken aback.

'This,' said the barman, holding out the card as if it was a small fish whose soul had three weeks earlier winged its way to the Land Where Fish are Eternally Blessed, 'we don't accept it.'

Ford wondered briefly whether to raise the fact that he didn't have any other means of payment on him, but decided for the moment to soldier on. The disembodied hand was now grasping his shoulder lightly but firmly between its finger and thumb.

'But you don't understand,' said Ford, his expression slowly ripening from a little taken abackness into rank incredulity. 'This is the American Express card. It is the finest way of settling bills known to man. Haven't you read their junk mail?'

The cheery quality of Ford's voice was beginning to grate on the barman's ears. It sounded like someone relentlessly playing the kazoo during one of the more sombre passages of a War Requiem.

One of the bones in Ford's shoulder began to grate against another one of the bones in his shoulder in a way which suggested that the hand had learnt the principles of pain from a highly skilled chiropractor. He hoped he could get this business settled before the hand started to grate one of the bones in his shoulder against any of the bones in different parts of his body. Luckily, the shoulder it was holding was not the one he had his satchel slung over.

The barman slid the card back across the bar at Ford.

'We have never,' he said with muted savagery, 'heard of this thing.'

This was hardly surprising.

Ford had only acquired it through a serious computer error towards the end of the fifteen years' sojourn he had spent on the planet Earth. Exactly how serious, the American Express company had got to know very rapidly, and the increasingly strident and panic-stricken demands of its debt collection department were only silenced by the unexpected demolition of the entire planet by the Vogons to make way for a new hyperspace bypass.

He had kept it ever since because he found it useful to carry a form of currency that no one would accept.

'Credit?' he said. 'Aaaargggh . . .'

These two words were usually coupled together in the Old Pink Dog Bar.

'I thought,' gasped Ford, 'that this was meant to be a class establishment . . .'

He glanced around at the motley collection of thugs, pimps and record company executives that skulked on the edges of the dim pools of light with which the dark shadows of the bar's inner recesses were pitted. They were all very deliberately looking in any direction but his now, carefully picking up the threads of their former conversations about murders, drug rings and music publishing deals. They knew what would happen now and didn't want to watch in case it put them off their drinks.

'You gonna die, boy,' the barman murmured quietly at Ford Prefect, and the evidence was on his side. The bar used to have one of those signs hanging up which said, 'Please don't ask for credit as a punch in the mouth often offends', but in the interest of strict accuracy this was altered to, 'Please don't ask for credit because having your throat torn out by a savage bird while a disembodied hand smashes your head against the bar often offends'. However, this made an unreadable mess of the notice, and anyway didn't have the same ring to it, so it was taken down again. It was felt that the story would get about of its own accord, and it had.

'Lemme look at the bill again,' said Ford. He picked it up and studied it thoughtfully under the malevolent gaze of the barman, and the equally malevolent gaze of the bird, which was currently gouging great furrows in the bar top with its talons.

It was a rather lengthy piece of paper.

At the bottom of it was a number which looked like one of those serial numbers you find on the underside of stereo sets which always takes so long to copy on to the registration form. He had, after all, been in the bar all day, he had been drinking a lot of stuff with bubbles in it, and he had bought an awful lot of rounds for all the pimps, thugs and record executives who suddenly couldn't remember who he was.

He cleared his throat rather quietly and patted his pockets. There was, as he knew, nothing in them. He rested his left hand lightly but firmly on the half-opened flap of his satchel. The disembodied hand renewed its pressure on his right shoulder.

'You see,' said the barman, and his face seemed to wobble evilly in front of Ford's, 'I have a reputation to think of. You see that, don't you?'

This is it, thought Ford. There was nothing else for it. He had obeyed the rules, he had made a bona fide attempt to pay his bill, it had been rejected. He was now in danger of his life.

'Well,' he said quietly, 'if it's your reputation . . .'

With a sudden flash of speed he opened his satchel and slapped down on the bar top his copy of *The Hitchhiker's Guide to the Galaxy* and the official card which said that he was a field researcher for the *Guide* and absolutely not allowed to do what he was now doing.

'Want a write up?'

The barman's face stopped in mid-wobble. The bird's talons stopped in mid-furrow. The hand slowly released its grip.

'That,' said the barman in a barely audible whisper, from between dry lips, 'will do nicely, sir.'

5

The Hitchhiker's Guide to the Galaxy is a powerful organ. Indeed, its influence is so prodigious that strict rules have had to be drawn up by its editorial staff to prevent its misuse. So none of its field researchers are allowed to accept any kind of services, discounts or preferential treatment of any kind in return for editorial favours unless:

a) they have made a bona fide attempt to pay for a service in the normal way;

b) their lives would be otherwise in danger;
c) they really want to.

Since invoking the third rule always involved giving the editor a cut, Ford always preferred to muck about with the first two.

He stepped out along the street, walking briskly.

The air was stifling, but he liked it because it was stifling city air, full of excitingly unpleasant smells, dangerous music and the distant sound of warring police tribes.

He carried his satchel with an easy swaying motion so that he could get a good swing at anybody who tried to take it from him without asking. It contained everything he owned, which at the moment wasn't much.

A limousine careered down the street, dodging between the piles of burning garbage, and frightening an old pack animal which lurched, screeching, out of its way, stumbled against the window of a herbal remedies shop, set off a wailing alarm, blundered off down the street, and then pretended to fall down the steps of a small pasta restaurant where it knew it would get photographed and fed.

Ford was walking north. He thought he was probably on his way to the spaceport, but he had thought that before. He knew he was going through that part of the city where people's plans often changed quite abruptly.

'Do you want to have a good time?' said a voice from a doorway.

'As far as I can tell,' said Ford, 'I'm having one. Thanks.'

'Are you rich?' said another.

This made Ford laugh.

He turned and opened his arms in a wide gesture. 'Do I *look* rich?' he said.

'Don't know,' said the girl. 'Maybe, maybe not. Maybe you'll get rich. I have a very special service for rich people . . .'

'Oh yes?' said Ford, intrigued but careful. 'And what's that?'

'I tell them it's OK to be rich.'

Gunfire erupted from a window high above them, but it was only a bass player getting shot for playing the wrong riff three times in a row, and bass players are two a penny in Han Dold City.

Ford stopped and peered into the dark doorway.

'You what?' he said.

The girl laughed and stepped forward a little out of the shadow. She was tall, and had that kind of self-possessed shyness which is a great trick if you can do it.

'It's my big number,' she said. 'I have a master's degree in Social Economics and can be very convincing. People love it. Especially in this city.'

'Goosnargh,' said Ford Prefect, which was a special Betelgeusian word he used when he knew he should say something but didn't know what it should be.

He sat on a step, took from his satchel a bottle of that Ol' Janx Spirit and a towel. He opened the bottle and wiped the top of it with the towel, which had the opposite effect to the one intended, in that the Ol' Janx Spirit instantly killed off millions of the germs which had been slowly building up quite a complex and enlightened civilization on the smellier patches of his towel.

'Want some?' he said, after he'd had a swig himself.

She shrugged and took the proffered bottle.

They sat for a while, peacefully listening to the clamour of burglar alarms in the next block.

'As it happens, I'm owed a lot of money,' said Ford,

'so if I ever get hold of it, can I come and see you then maybe?'

'Sure, I'll be here,' said the girl. 'So how much is a lot?'

'Fifteen years' back pay.'

'For?'

'Writing two words.'

'Zarquon,' said the girl. 'Which one took the time?'

'The first one. Once I'd got that the second one just came one afternoon after lunch.'

A huge electronic drum kit hurtled through the window high above them and smashed itself to bits in the street in front of them.

It soon became apparent that some of the burglar alarms on the next block had been deliberately set off by one police tribe in order to lay an ambush for the other. Cars with screaming sirens converged on the area, only to find themselves being picked off by copters which came thudding through the air between the city's mountainous tower blocks.

'In fact,' said Ford, having to shout now above the din, 'it wasn't quite like that. I wrote an awful lot, but they just cut it down.'

He took his copy of the *Guide* back out of his satchel.

'Then the planet got demolished,' he shouted. 'Really worthwhile job, eh? They've still got to pay me, though.'

'You work for that thing?' the girl yelled back.

'Yeah.'

'Good number.'

'You want to see the stuff I wrote?' he shouted. 'Before it gets erased? The new revisions are due to be released tonight over the net. Someone must have found out that the planet I spent fifteen years on has been demolished by now. They missed it on the last few revisions, but it can't escape their notice for ever.'

'It's getting impossible to talk, isn't it?'

'What?'

She shrugged and pointed upwards.

There was a copter above them now which seemed to be involved in a side skirmish with the band upstairs. Smoke was billowing from the building. The sound engineer was hanging out of the window by his fingertips, and a maddened guitarist was beating on his fingers with a burning guitar. The helicopter was firing at all of them.

'Can we move?'

They wandered down the street, away from the noise. They ran into a street theatre group which tried to do a short play for them about the problems of the inner city, but then gave up and disappeared into the small restaurant most recently patronized by the pack animal.

All the time, Ford was poking at the interface panel of the *Guide*. They ducked into an alleyway. Ford squatted on a garbage can while information began to flood over the screen of the *Guide*.

He located his entry.

'Earth: Mostly harmless.'

Almost immediately the screen became a mass of system messages.

'Here it comes,' he said.

'Please wait,' said the messages. *'Entries are being updated over the Sub-Etha Net. This entry is being revised. The system will be down for ten seconds.'*

At the end of the alley a steel grey limousine crawled past.

'Hey look,' said the girl, 'if you get paid, look me up. I'm a working girl, and there are people over there who need me. I gotta go.'

She brushed aside Ford's half-articulated protests, and left him sitting dejectedly on his garbage can preparing to watch a large swathe of his working life being swept away electronically into the ether.

Out in the street things had calmed down a little. The police battle had moved off to other sectors of the city, the few surviving members of the rock band had agreed to recognize their musical differences and pursue solo careers, the street theatre group were re-emerging from the pasta restaurant with the pack animal, telling it they would take it to a bar they knew where it would be treated with a little respect, and a little way further on the steel grey limousine was parked silently by the kerbside.

The girl hurried towards it.

* * *

Behind her, in the darkness of the alley, a green flickering glow was bathing Ford Prefect's face, and his eyes were slowly widening in astonishment.

For where he had expected to find nothing, an erased, closed-off entry, there was instead a continuous stream of data – text, diagrams, figures and images, moving descriptions of surf on Australian beaches, yoghurt on Greek islands, restaurants to avoid in Los Angeles, currency deals to avoid in Istanbul, weather to avoid in London, bars to go everywhere. Pages and pages of it. It was all there, everything he had written.

With a deepening frown of blank incomprehension he went backwards and forwards through it, stopping here and there at various entries.

'Tips for aliens in New York:

'Land anywhere, Central Park, anywhere. No one will care, or indeed even notice.

'Surviving: Get a job as a cab driver immediately. A cab driver's job is to drive people anywhere they want to go in big yellow machines called taxis. Don't worry if you don't

know how the machine works and you can't speak the language, don't understand the geography or indeed the basic physics of the area, and have large green antennae growing out of your head. Believe me, this is the best way of staying inconspicuous.

'If your body is really weird try showing it to people in the streets for money.

'Amphibious life forms from any of the worlds in the Swulling, Noxios or Nausalia systems will particularly enjoy the East River, which is said to be richer in those lovely life-giving nutrients than the finest and most virulent laboratory slime yet achieved.

'Having fun: This is the big section. It is impossible to have more fun without electrocuting your pleasure centres . . .'

Ford flipped the switch which he saw was now marked 'Mode Execute Ready' instead of the now old-fashioned 'Access Standby' which had so long ago replaced the appallingly stone-age 'Off'.

This was a planet he had seen completely destroyed, seen with his own two eyes or rather, blinded as he had been by the hellish disruption of air and light, felt with his own two feet as the ground had started to pound at him like a hammer, bucking, roaring, gripped by tidal waves of energy pouring out of the loathsome yellow Vogon ships. And then at last, five seconds after the moment he had determined as being the last possible moment had already passed, the gently swinging nausea of dematerialization as he and Arthur Dent had been beamed up through the atmosphere like a sports broadcast.

There was no mistake, there couldn't have been. The Earth had definitely been destroyed. Definitely, definitely. Boiled away into space.

And yet here – he activated the *Guide* again – was his own entry on how you would set about having a good time in Bournemouth, Dorset, England, which he had always prided himself on as being one of the most baroque pieces of invention he had ever delivered. He read it again and shook his head in sheer wonder.

Suddenly he realized what the answer to the problem was, and it was this, that something very weird was happening; and if something very weird was happening, he thought, he wanted it to be happening to him.

He stashed the *Guide* back in his satchel and hurried out on to the street again.

Walking north again he passed a steel grey limousine parked by the kerbside, and from a nearby doorway he heard a soft voice saying, 'It's OK, honey, it's really OK, you got to learn to feel good about it. Look at the way the whole economy is structured . . .'

Ford grinned, detoured round the next block which was now in flames, found a police helicopter which was standing unattended in the street, broke into it, strapped himself in, crossed his fingers and sent it hurtling inexpertly into the sky.

He weaved terrifyingly up through the canyoned walls of the city, and once clear of them hurtled through the black and red pall of smoke which hung permanently above it.

Ten minutes later, with all the copter's sirens blaring and its rapid-fire cannon blasting at random into the clouds, Ford Prefect brought it careering down among the gantries and landing lights at Han Dold spaceport, where it settled like a gigantic, startled and very noisy gnat.

Since he hadn't damaged it too much he was able to trade it in for a first-class ticket on the next ship leaving the system, and settled into one of its huge, voluptuous body-hugging seats.

This was going to be fun, he thought to himself, as

the ship blinked silently across the insane distances of deep space and the cabin service got into its full extravagant swing.

'Yes please,' he said to the cabin attendants whenever they glided up to offer him anything at all.

He smiled with a curious kind of manic joy as he flipped again through the mysteriously reinstated entry on the planet Earth. He had a major piece of unfinished business that he would now be able to attend to, and was terribly pleased that life had suddenly furnished him with a serious goal to achieve.

It suddenly occured to him to wonder where Arthur Dent was, and if he knew.

* * *

Arthur Dent was one thousand, four hundred and thirty-seven light-years away in a Saab, and anxious.

Behind him in the back seat was a girl who had made him crack his head on the door as he climbed in. He didn't know if it was just because she was the first female of his own species that he had laid eyes on in years, or what it was, but he felt stupefied with, with ... This is absurd, he told himself. Calm down, he told himself. You are not, he continued to himself in the firmest internal voice he could muster, in a fit and rational state. You have just hitch hiked over a hundred thousand light-years across the galaxy, you are very tired, a little confused and extremely vulnerable. Relax, don't panic, concentrate on breathing deeply.

He twisted round in his seat.

'Are you *sure* she's all right?' he said again.

Beyond the fact that she was, to him, heart-thumpingly beautiful, he could make out very little, how tall she was, how old she was, the exact shading of her hair.

And nor could he ask her anything about herself because, sadly, she was completely unconscious.

'She's just drugged,' said her brother, shrugging, not moving his eyes from the road ahead.

'And that's all right, is it?' said Arthur, in alarm.

'Suits me,' he said.

'Ah,' said Arthur. 'Er,' he added after a moment's thought.

The conversation so far had been going astoundingly badly.

After an initial flurry of opening hellos, he and Russell – the wonderful girl's brother's name was Russell, a name which, to Arthur's mind, always suggested burly men with blond moustaches and blow-dried hair, who would at the slightest provocation start wearing velvet tuxedos and frilly shirtfronts and would then have to be forcibly restrained from commentating on snooker matches – had quickly discovered they didn't like each other at all.

Russell was a burly man. He had a blond moustache. His hair was fine and blow dried. To be fair to him – though Arthur didn't see any necessity for this beyond the sheer mental exercise of it – he, Arthur, was looking pretty grim himself. A man can't cross a hundred thousand light-years, mostly in other people's baggage compartments, without beginning to fray a little, and Arthur had frayed a lot.

'She's not a junkie,' said Russell suddenly, as if he clearly thought that someone else in the car might be. 'She's under sedation.'

'But that's terrible,' said Arthur, twisting round to look at her again. She seemed to stir slightly and her head slipped sideways on her shoulder. Her dark hair fell across her face, obscuring it.

'What's the matter with her, is she ill?'

'No,' said Russell, 'merely barking mad.'

'What?' said Arthur, horrified.

'Loopy, completely bananas. I'm taking her back to the hospital and telling them to have another go. They let her out while she still thought she was a hedgehog.'

'A *hedgehog?*'

Russell hooted his horn fiercely at a car that came round the corner towards them halfway on to their side of the road, making them swerve. The anger seemed to make him feel better.

'Well, maybe not a hedgehog,' he said after he'd settled down again. 'Though it would probably be simpler to deal with if she did. If somebody thinks they're a hedgehog, presumably you just give 'em a mirror and a few pictures of hedgehogs and tell them to sort it out for themselves, come down again when they feel better. At least medical science could deal with it, that's the point. Seems that's not good enough for Fenny, though.'

'Fenny . . .?'

'You know what I got her for Christmas?'

'Well, no.'

'*Black's Medical Dictionary*.'

'Nice present.'

'I thought so. Thousands of diseases in it, all in alphabetical order.'

'You say her name is Fenny?'

'Yeah. Take your pick, I said. Anything in here can be dealt with. The proper drugs can be prescribed. But no, she has to have something different. Just to make life difficult. She was like that at school, you know.'

'Was she?'

'She was. Fell over playing hockey and broke a bone nobody had ever heard of.'

'I can see how that would be irritating,' said Arthur

doubtfully. He was rather disappointed to discover her name was Fenny. It was a rather silly, dispiriting name, such as an unlovely maiden aunt might vote herself if she couldn't sustain the name Fenella properly.

'Not that I wasn't sympathetic,' continued Russell, 'but it did get a bit irritating. She was limping for months.'

He slowed down.

'This is your turning, isn't it?'

'Ah, no,' said Arthur, 'five miles further on. If that's all right.'

'OK,' said Russell after a very tiny pause to indicate that it wasn't, and speeded up again.

It was in fact Arthur's turning, but he couldn't leave without finding out something more about this girl who seemed to have taken such a grip on his mind without even waking up. He could take either of the next two turnings.

They led back to the village that had been his home, though what he would find there he hesitated to imagine. Familiar landmarks had been flitting by, ghostlike, in the dark, giving rise to the shudders that only very very normal things can create, when seen where the mind is unprepared for them, and in an unfamiliar light.

By his own personal time scale, so far as he could estimate it, living as he had been under the alien rotations of distant suns, it was eight years since he had left, but what time had passed here he could hardly guess. Indeed, what events had passed were beyond his exhausted comprehension because this planet, his home, should not be here.

Eight years ago, at lunchtime, this planet had been demolished, utterly destroyed, by the huge yellow Vogon ships which had hung in the lunchtime sky as if the law of gravity was no more than a local regulation, and breaking it no more than a parking offence.

'Delusions,' said Russell.

'What?' said Arthur, started out of his train of thought.

'She says she suffers from strange delusions that she's living in the real world. It's no good telling her that she *is* living in the real world because she just says that's why the delusions are so strange. Don't know about you, but I find that kind of conversation pretty exhausting. Give her the tablets and piss off for a beer is my answer. I mean you can only muck about so much can't you?'

Arthur frowned, not for the first time.

'Well . . .'

'And all this dreams and nightmare stuff. And the doctors going on about strange jumps in her brainwave patterns.'

'Jumps?'

'This,' said Fenny.

Arthur whirled round in his seat and stared into her suddenly open but utterly vacant eyes. Whatever she was looking at wasn't in the car. Her eyes fluttered, her head jerked once, and then she was sleeping peacefully.

'What did she say?' he asked anxiously.

'She said "this".'

'This what?'

'This what? How the heck should I know? This hedgehog, that chimney pot, the other pair of Don Alfonso's tweezers. She's barking mad, I thought I'd mentioned that.'

'You don't seem to care very much.' Arthur tried to say it as matter-of-factly as possible but it didn't seem to work.

'Look, buster . . .'

'OK, I'm sorry. It's none of my business. I didn't mean it to sound like that,' said Arthur. 'I know you care a lot, obviously,' he added, lying. 'I know that you have to deal with it somehow. You'll have to excuse me. I just hitched from the other side of the Horsehead Nebula.'

He stared furiously out of the window.

He was astonished that of all the sensations fighting for room in his head on this night as he returned to the home that he thought had vanished into oblivion for ever, the one that was compelling him was an obsession with this bizarre girl of whom he knew nothing other than that she had said 'this' to him, and that he wouldn't wish her brother on a Vogon.

'So, er, what were the jumps, these jumps you mentioned?' he went on to say as quickly as he could.

'Look, this is my sister, I don't even know why I'm talking to you about . . .'

'OK, I'm sorry. Perhaps you'd better let me out. This is . . .'

At the moment he said it, it became impossible, because the storm which had passed them by suddenly erupted again. Lightning belted through the sky, and someone seemed to be pouring something which closely resembled the Atlantic Ocean over them through a sieve.

Russell swore and steered intently for a few seconds as the sky blattered at them. He worked out his anger by rashly accelerating to pass a lorry marked 'McKenna's All-Weather Haulage'. The tension eased as the rain subsided.

'It started with all that business of the CIA agent they found in the reservoir, when everybody had all the hallucinations and everything, you remember?'

Arthur wondered for a moment whether to mention

again that he had just hitch hiked back from the other side of the Horsehead Nebula and was for this and various other related and astounding reasons a little out of touch with recent events, but he decided it would only confuse matters further.

'No,' he said.

'That was the moment she cracked up. She was in a café somewhere. Rickmansworth. Don't know what she was doing there, but that was where she cracked up. Apparently she stood up, calmly announced that she had undergone some extraordinary revelation or something, wobbled a bit, looked confused, and finally collapsed screaming into an egg sandwich.'

Arthur winced. 'I'm very sorry to hear that,' he said a little stiffly.

Russell made a sort of grumping noise.

'So what,' said Arthur in an attempt to piece things together, 'was the CIA agent doing in the reservoir?'

'Bobbing up and down, of course. He was dead.'

'But what . . .'

'Come on, you remember all that stuff. The hallucinations. Everyone said it was a cock up, the CIA trying experiments into drug warfare or something. Some crackpot theory that instead of invading a country it would be much cheaper and more effective to make everyone *think* they'd been invaded.'

'What hallucinations were those exactly . . . ?' said Arthur in a rather quiet voice.

'What do you mean, what hallucinations? I'm talking about all that stuff with the big yellow ships, everyone going crazy and saying we're going to die, and then pop, they vanished as the effect wore off. The CIA denied it which meant it must be true.'

Arthur's head went a little swimmy. His hand grabbed at something to steady himself, and gripped it tightly. His mouth made little opening and closing movements as if it was on his mind to say something, but nothing emerged.

'Anyway,' continued Russell, 'whatever drug it was it didn't seem to wear off so fast with Fenny. I was all for suing the CIA, but a lawyer friend of mine said it would be like trying to attack a lunatic asylum with a banana, so . . .' He shrugged.

'The Vogon . . .' squeaked Arthur. 'The yellow ships . . . *vanished*?'

'Well, of course they did, they were hallucinations,' said Russell, and looked at Arthur oddly. 'You trying to say you don't remember any of this? Where have you been, for Heaven's sake?'

This was, to Arthur, such an astonishingly good question that he half-leapt out of his seat with shock.

'Christ!!!' yelled Russell, fighting to control the car which was suddenly trying to skid. He pulled it out of the path of an oncoming lorry and swerved up on to a grass bank. As the car lurched to a halt, the girl in the back was thrown against Russell's seat and collapsed awkwardly.

Arthur twisted round in horror.

'Is she all right?' he blurted out.

Russell swept his hands angrily back through his blow-dried hair. He tugged at his blond moustache. He turned to Arthur.

'Would you please,' he said, 'let go of the handbrake?'

6

From here it was a four-mile walk to his village: a mile further to the turning, to which the abominable Russell had now fiercely declined to take him, and from there a further three miles of winding country lane.

The Saab seethed off into the night. Arthur watched it go, as stunned as a man might be who, having believed himself to be totally blind for five years, suddenly discovers that he had merely been wearing too large a hat.

He shook his head sharply in the hope that it might dislodge some salient fact which would fall into place and make sense of an otherwise utterly bewildering Universe, but since the salient fact, if there was one, entirely failed to do this, he set off up the road again, hoping that a good vigorous walk, and maybe even some good painful blisters, would help to reassure him of his own existence at least, if not his sanity.

It was 10.30 when he arrived, a fact he discovered from the steamed and greasy window of the Horse and Groom pub, in which there had hung for many years a battered old Guinness clock which featured a picture of an emu with a pint glass jammed rather amusingly down its throat.

This was the pub at which he had passed the fateful lunchtime during which first his house and then the entire planet Earth had been demolished, or rather had seemed to be demolished. No, damn it, *had* been demolished, because if it hadn't then where the bloody heck had he *been* for the last eight years, and how had he got there if not in one of the big yellow Vogon ships which the appalling Russell had just been telling him were merely drug-induced hallucinations, and yet if it *had* been demolished, what was he currently standing on . . .?

He jammed the brake on this line of thought because it wasn't going to get him any further than it had the last twenty times he'd been over it.

He started again.

This was the pub at which he had passed the fateful lunchtime during which whatever it was had happened that he was going to sort out later had happened, and . . .

It still didn't make sense.

He started again.

This was the pub in which . . .

This was a pub.

Pubs served drinks and he couldn't half do with one.

Satisfied that his jumbled thought processes had at last arrived at a conclusion, and a conclusion he was happy with, even if it wasn't the one he had set out to achieve, he strode towards the door.

And stopped.

A small black wire-haired terrier ran out from behind a low wall and then, catching sight of Arthur, began to snarl.

Now Arthur knew this dog, and he knew it well. It belonged to an advertising friend of his, and was called Know-Nothing Bozo because the way its hair stood up on its head reminded people of the President of the United States of America, and the dog knew Arthur, or at least should do. It was a stupid dog, could not even read an autocue, which was why some people had protested about its name, but it should at least have been able to recognize Arthur instead of standing there, hackles raised, as if Arthur was the most fearful apparition ever to intrude upon its feeble-witted life.

This prompted Arthur to go and peer at the window again, this time with an eye not for the asphyxiating emu but for himself.

Seeing himself for the first time suddenly in a familiar context, he had to admit that the dog had a point.

He looked a lot like something a farmer would use to scare birds with, and there was no doubt but that to go into the pub in his present condition would excite comment of a raucous kind, and worse still, there would doubtless be several people in there at the moment whom he knew, all of whom would be bound to bombard him with questions which, at the moment, he felt ill-equipped to deal with.

Will Smithers, for instance, the owner of Know-Nothing Bozo the Non-Wonder Dog, an animal so stupid that it had been sacked from one of Will's own commercials for being incapable of knowing which dog food it was supposed to prefer, despite the fact that the meat in all the other bowls had had engine oil poured over it.

Will would definitely be in there. Here was his dog, there was his car, a grey Porsche 928S with a sign in the back window which read, 'My other car is also a Porsche.' Damn him.

He stared at it and realized that he had just learned something he hadn't known before.

Will Smithers, like most of the overpaid and under-scrupulous bastards Arthur knew in advertising made a point of changing his car every August so that he could tell people his accountant made him do it, though the truth was that his accountant was trying like hell to stop him, what with all the alimony he had to pay, and so on – and this was the same car Arthur remembered him having before. The number plate proclaimed its year.

Given that it was now winter, and that the event which had caused Arthur so much trouble eight of his personal years ago had occurred at the beginning of September, less than six or seven months could have passed here.

He stood terribly still for a moment and let Know-Nothing Bozo jump up and down yapping at him. He was suddenly stunned by a realization he could no longer avoid, which was this: he was now an alien on his own world. Try as they might, no one was even going to be *able* to believe his story. Not only did it sound perfectly potty, but it was flatly contradicted by the simplest observable facts.

Was this *really* the Earth? Was there the slightest possibility that he had made some extraordinary mistake?

The pub in front of him was unbearably familiar to him in every detail – every brick, every piece of peeling paint; and inside he could sense its familiar stuffy, noisy warmth, its exposed beams, its unauthentic cast-iron light fittings, its bar sticky with beer that people he knew had put their elbows in, overlooked by cardboard cutouts of girls with packets of peanuts stapled all over their breasts. It was all the stuff of his home, his world.

He even knew this blasted dog.

'Hey, Know-Nothing!'

The sound of Will Smithers' voice meant he had to decide what to do quickly. If he stood his ground he would be discovered and the whole circus would begin. To hide would only postpone the moment, and it was bitterly cold now.

The fact that it was Will made the choice easier. It wasn't that Arthur disliked him as such – Will was quite fun. It was just that he was fun in such an exhausting way because, being in advertising, he always wanted you to know how much fun he was having and where he had got his jacket from.

Mindful of this, Arthur hid behind a van.

'Hey, Know-Nothing, what's up?'

The door opened and Will came out, wearing a leather flying jacket that he'd got a mate of his at the Road Research Laboratory to crash a car into specially, in order to get that battered look. Know-Nothing yelped with delight and, having got the attention it wanted, was happy to forget Arthur.

Will was with some friends, and they had a game they played with the dog.

'Commies!' they all shouted at the dog in chorus. 'Commies, commies, commies!!!'

The dog went berserk with barking, prancing up and down, yapping its little heart out, beside itself in transports of ecstatic rage. They all laughed and cheered it on, then gradually dispersed to their various cars and disappeared into the night.

Well, that clears one thing up, thought Arthur from behind the van, this is quite definitely the planet I remember.

7

His house was still there.

How or why, he had no idea. He had decided to go and have a look while he was waiting for the pub to empty, so that he could go and ask the landlord for a bed for the night when everyone else had gone. And there it was.

He hurriedly let himself in with a key he kept under a stone frog in the garden, because, astoundingly, the phone was ringing.

He had heard it faintly all the way up the lane and had started to run as soon as he realized where the sound was coming from.

The door had to be forced open because of the astonishing accumulation of junk mail on the doormat. It jammed itself stuck on what he would later discover were fourteen identical, personally addressed invitations to apply for a credit card he already had, seventeen identical threatening letters for non-payment of bills on a credit card he didn't have, thirty-three identical letters saying that he personally had been specially selected as a man of taste and discrimination who knew what he wanted and where he was going in today's sophisticated jet-setting world and would he therefore like to buy some grotty wallet, and also a dead tabby kitten.

He rammed himself through the relatively narrow opening afforded by all this, stumbled through a pile of wine offers that no discriminating connoisseur would want to miss, slithered over a heap of beach villa holidays, blundered up the dark stairs to his bedroom and got to the phone just as it stopped ringing.

He collapsed, panting, on to his cold, musty-smelling bed and for a few minutes stopped trying to prevent the world from spinning round his head in the way it obviously wanted to.

When it had enjoyed its little spin and had calmed down a bit, Arthur reached out for the bedside light, not expecting it to come on. To his surprise it did. This appealed to Arthur's sense of logic. Since the Electricity Board cut him off without fail every time he paid his bill, it seemed only reasonable that they should leave him connected when he didn't. Sending them money obviously only drew attention to yourself.

The room was much as he had left it, i.e. festeringly untidy, though the effect was muted a little by a thick layer of dust. Half-read books and magazines nestled amongst piles of half-used towels. Half pairs of socks reclined in half-drunk cups of coffee. What was once a half-eaten sandwich had now half-turned into something that Arthur entirely didn't want to know about. Bung a fork of lightning through this lot, he thought to himself, and you'd start the evolution of life off all over again.

There was only one thing in the room that was different.

For a moment or so he couldn't see what the one thing that was different was, because it too was covered in a film of disgusting dust. Then his eyes caught it and stopped.

It was next to a battered old television on which it was only possible to watch Open University Study Courses, because if it tried to show anything more exciting it would break down.

It was a box.

Arthur pushed himself up on his elbows and peered at it.

It was a grey box, with a kind of dull lustre to it. It was a cubic grey box, just over a foot on a side. It was tied with a single grey ribbon, knotted into a neat bow on the top.

He got up, walked over and touched it in surprise. Whatever it was was clearly gift-wrapped, neatly and beautifully, and was waiting for him to open it.

Cautiously, he picked it up and carried it back to the bed. He brushed the dust off the top and loosened the ribbon. The top of the box was a lid, with a flap tucked into the body of the box.

He untucked it and looked into the box. In it was a glass globe, nestling in fine grey tissue paper. He drew it out, carefully. It wasn't a proper globe because it was open at the bottom, or, as Arthur realized turning it over, at the top, with a thick rim. It was a bowl. A fish bowl.

It was made of the most wonderful glass, perfectly transparent, yet with an extraordinary – silver-grey quality as if crystal and slate had gone into its making.

Arthur slowly turned it over and over in his hands. It was one of the most beautiful objects he had ever seen, but he was entirely perplexed by it. He looked into the box, but other than the tissue paper there was nothing. On the outside of the box there was nothing.

He turned the bowl round again. It was wonderful. It was exquisite. But it was a fish bowl.

He tapped it with his thumbnail and it rang with a deep and glorious chime which was sustained for longer than seemed possible, and when at last it faded seemed not to die away but to drift off into other worlds, as into a deep sea dream.

Entranced, Arthur turned it round yet again, and this time the light from the dusty little bedside lamp caught it at a different angle and glittered on some fine abrasions on the fish bowl's surface. He held it up, adjusting the angle to the light, and suddenly saw clearly the finely engraved shapes of words shadowed on the glass.

'So Long,' they said, 'and Thanks . . .'

And that was all. He blinked, and understood nothing.

For fully five more minutes he turned the object

round and around, held it to the light at different angles, tapped it for its mesmerizing chime and pondered on the meaning of the shadowy letters but could find none. Finally he stood up, filled the bowl with water from the tap and put it back on the table next to the television. He shook the little Babel fish from his ear and dropped it, wriggling, into the bowl. He wouldn't be needing it any more, except for watching foreign movies.

He returned to lie on his bed, and turned out the light.

He lay still and quiet. He absorbed the enveloping darkness, slowly relaxed his limbs from end to end, eased and regulated his breathing, gradually cleared his mind of all thought, closed his eyes and was completely incapable of getting to sleep.

* * *

The night was uneasy with rain. The rain clouds themselves had now moved on and were currently concentrating their attention on a small transport café just outside Bournemouth, but the sky through which they had passed had been disturbed by them and now wore a damply ruffled air, as if it didn't know what else it might not do if further provoked.

The moon was out in a watery way. It looked like a ball of paper from the back pocket of jeans that have just come out of the washing machine, and which only time and ironing would tell if it was an old shopping list or a five-pound note.

The wind flicked about a little, like the tail of a horse that's trying to decide what sort of mood it's in tonight, and a bell somewhere chimed midnight.

A skylight creaked open.

It was stiff and had to be jiggled and persuaded a little because the frame was slightly rotten and the hinge had at some time in its life been rather sensibly painted over, but eventually it was open.

A strut was found to prop it and a figure struggled out into the narrow gully between the opposing pitches of the roof.

It stood and watched the sky in silence.

The figure was completely unrecognizable as the wild-looking creature who had burst crazily into the cottage a little over an hour ago. Gone was the ragged threadbare dressing gown, smeared with the mud of a hundred worlds, stained with junk food condiment from a hundred grimy spaceports, gone was the tangled mane of hair, gone the long and knotted beard, flourishing ecosystem and all.

Instead, there was Arthur Dent the smooth and casual, in corduroys and a chunky sweater. His hair was cropped and washed, his chin clean shaven. Only the eyes still said that whatever it was the Universe thought it was doing to him, he would still like it please to stop.

They were not the same eyes with which he had last looked out at this particular scene, and the brain which interpreted the images the eyes resolved was not the same brain. There had been no surgery involved, just the continual wrenching of experience.

The night seemed like an alive thing to him at this moment, the dark earth around him a being in which he was rooted.

He could feel like a tingle on distant nerve ends the flood of a far river, the roll of invisible hills, the knot of heavy rainclouds parked somewhere away to the south.

He could sense, too, the thrill of being a tree, which was something he hadn't expected. He knew that it felt good to curl your toes in the earth, but he'd never realized it could feel quite as good as that. He could sense an almost unseemly wave of pleasure reaching out to him all the way from the New Forest. He must try this summer, he thought, and see what having leaves felt like.

From another direction he felt the sensation of being a sheep startled by a flying saucer, but it was virtually indistinguishable from the feeling of being a sheep startled by anything else it ever encountered, for they were creatures who learned very little on their journey through life, and would be startled to see the sun rising in the morning, and astonished by all the green stuff in the fields.

He was surprised to find he could feel the sheep being startled by the sun that morning, and the morning before, and being startled by a clump of trees the day before that. He could go further and further back, but it got dull because all it consisted of was sheep being startled by things they'd been startled by the day before.

He left the sheep and let his mind drift outwards sleepily in developing ripples. It felt the presence of other minds, hundreds of them, thousands in a web, some sleepy, some sleeping, some terribly excited, one fractured.

One fractured.

He passed it fleetingly and tried to feel for it again, but it eluded him like the other card with an apple on it in Pelmanism. He felt a spasm of excitement because he knew instinctively who it was, or at least knew who it was he wanted it to be, and once you know what it is you want to be true, instinct is a very useful device for enabling you to know that it is.

He instinctively knew that it was Fenny and that he wanted to find her; but he could not. By straining too much for it, he could feel he was losing this strange new faculty, so he relaxed the search and let his mind wander more easily once more.

And again, he felt the fracture.

Again he couldn't find it. This time, whatever his instinct was busy telling him it was all right to believe, he wasn't certain that it was Fenny or – perhaps it was a different fracture this time. It had the same disjointed quality but it seemed a more general feeling of fracture, deeper, not a single mind, maybe not a mind at all. It was different.

He let his mind sink slowly and widely into the Earth, rippling, seeping, sinking.

He was following the Earth through its days, drifting with the rhythms of its myriad pulses, seeping through the webs of its life, swelling with its tides, turning with its weight. Always the fracture kept returning, a dull disjointed distant ache.

And now he was flying through a land of light; the light was time, the tides of it were days receding. The fracture he had sensed, the second fracture, lay in the distance before him across the land, the thickness of a single hair across the dreaming landscape of the days of Earth.

And suddenly he was upon it.

He danced dizzily over the edge as the dreamland dropped sheer away beneath him, a stupefying precipice into nothing, him wildly twisting, clawing at nothing, flailing in horrifying space, spinning, falling.

Across the jagged chasm had been another land, another time, an older world, not fractured from, but hardly joined: two Earths. He woke.

A cold breeze brushed the feverish sweat standing on his forehead. The nightmare was spent and so, he felt, was he. His shoulders dropped, he gently rubbed his eyes with the tips of his fingers. At last he was sleepy as well as very tired. As to what it meant, if it meant anything at all, he would think about in the morning; for now he would go to bed and sleep. His own bed, his own sleep.

He could see his house in the distance and wondered why this was. It was silhouetted against the moonlight and he recognized its rather dull blockish shape. He looked about him and noticed that he was about eighteen inches above the rose bushes of one of his neighbours, John Ainsworth. His rose bushes were carefully tended, pruned back for the winter, strapped to canes and labelled, and Arthur wondered what he was doing above them. He wondered what was holding him there, and when he discovered that nothing was holding him there he crashed awkwardly to the ground.

He picked himself up, brushed himself down and hobbled back to his house on a sprained ankle. He undressed and toppled into bed.

While he was asleep the phone rang again. It rang for fully fifteen minutes and caused him to turn over twice. It never, however, stood a chance of waking him up.

8

Arthur awoke feeling wonderful, absolutely fabulous, refreshed, overjoyed to be home, bouncing with energy, hardly disappointed at all to discover it was the middle of February.

He almost danced to the fridge, found the three least hairy things in it, put them on a plate and watched them intently for two minutes. Since they made no attempt to move within that time he called them breakfast and ate them. Between them they killed a virulent space disease he'd picked up without knowing it in the Flargathon Gas Swamps a few days earlier, which otherwise would have killed off half the population of the Western Hemisphere, blinded the other half and driven everyone else psychotic and sterile, so the Earth was lucky there.

He felt strong, he felt healthy. He vigorously cleared away the junk mail with a spade and then buried the cat.

Just as he was finishing that, the phone went, but he let it ring while he maintained a moment's respectful silence. Whoever it was would ring back if it was important.

He kicked the mud off his shoes and went back inside.

There had been a small number of significant letters in the piles of junk – some documents from the council, dated three years earlier, relating to the proposed demolition of his house, and some other letters about the setting up of a public inquiry into the whole bypass scheme in the area; there was also an old letter from Greenpeace, the ecological pressure group to which he occasionally made contributions, asking for help with their scheme to release dolphins and orcas from captivity, and some postcards from friends vaguely complaining that he never got in touch these days.

He collected these together and put them in a cardboard file which he marked 'Things To Do'. Since he was feeling so vigorous and dynamic that morning, he even added the word 'Urgent!'

He unpacked his towel and another few odd bits and pieces from the plastic bag he had acquired at the Port Brasta Mega-Market. The slogan on the side was a clever and elaborate pun in Lingua Centauri which was completely incomprehensible in any other language and therefore entirely pointless for a duty free shop at a spaceport. The bag also had a hole in it so he threw it away.

He realized with a sudden twinge that something else must have dropped out in the small spacecraft that had brought him to Earth, kindly going out of its way to drop him right beside the A303. He had lost his battered and spaceworn copy of the thing which had helped him find his way across the unbelievable wastes of space he had traversed. He had lost *The Hitchhiker's Guide to the Galaxy.*

Well, he told himself, this time I really won't be needing it again.

He had some calls to make.

He had decided how to deal with the mass of contradictions his return journey precipitated, which was that he would simply brazen it out.

He phoned the BBC and asked to be put through to his department head.

'Oh, hello, Arthur Dent here. Look, sorry I haven't been in for six months but I've gone mad.'

'Oh, not to worry. Thought it was probably something like that. Happens here all the time. How soon can we expect you?'

'When do hedgehogs stop hibernating?'

'Sometime in spring, I think.'

'I'll be in shortly after that.'

'Rightyho.'

He flipped through the Yellow Pages and made a short list of numbers to try.

'Oh hello, is that the Old Elms Hospital? Yes, I was just phoning to see if I could have a word with Fenella, er . . . Fenella – Good Lord, silly me, I'll forget my own name next, er, Fenella – isn't this ridiculous? Patient of yours, dark-haired girl, came in last night . . .'

'I'm afraid we don't have any patients called Fenella.'

'Oh, don't you? I meant Fiona, of course, we just call her Fen . . .'

'I'm sorry, goodbye.'

Click.

Six conversations along these lines began to take their toll on his mood of vigorous, dynamic optimism, and he decided that before it deserted him entirely he would take it down to the pub and parade it a little.

He had had the perfect idea for explaining away every inexplicable weirdness about himself at a stroke, and he whistled to himself as he pushed open the door which had so daunted him last night.

'Arthur!!!!'

He grinned cheerfully at the boggling eyes that stared at him from all corners of the pub, and told them all what a wonderful time he'd had in Southern California.

9

He accepted another pint and took a pull at it.

'Of course, I had my own personal alchemist too.'

'You what?'

He was getting silly and he knew it. Exuberance and Hall and Woodhouse best bitter was a mixture to be wary of, but one of the first effects it has is to stop you being wary of things, and the point at which Arthur should have stopped and explained no more was the point at which he started instead to get inventive.

'Oh yes,' he insisted with a happy glazed smile. 'It's why I've lost so much weight.'

'What?' said his audience.

'Oh yes,' he said again. 'The Californians have rediscovered alchemy. Oh yes.'

He smiled again.

'Only,' he said, 'it's in a much more useful form than that which in . . .' He paused thoughtfully to let a little grammar assemble in his head. 'In which the ancients used to practise it. Or at least,' he added, 'failed to practise it. They couldn't get it to work, you know. Nostradamus and that lot. Couldn't cut it.'

'Nostradamus?' said one of his audience.

'I didn't think he was an alchemist,' said another.

'I thought,' said a third, 'he was a seer.'

'He became a seer,' said Arthur to his audience, the component parts of which were beginning to bob and blur a little, 'because he was such a lousy alchemist. You should know that.'

He took another pull at his beer. It was something he had not tasted for eight years. He tasted it and tasted it.

'What has alchemy got to do,' asked a bit of the audience, 'with losing weight?'

'I'm glad you asked that,' said Arthur. 'Very glad. And I will now tell you what the connection is between . . .' He paused. 'Between those two things. The things you mentioned. I'll tell you.'

He paused and manoeuvred his thoughts. It was like watching oil tankers doing three-point turns in the English Channel.

'They've discovered how to turn excess body fat into gold,' he said, in a sudden blurt of coherence.

'You're kidding.'

'Oh yes,' he said, 'no,' he corrected himself, 'they have.'

He rounded on the doubting part of his audience, which was all of it, and so it took a little while to round on it completely.

'Have you *been* to California?' he demanded. 'Do you *know* the sort of stuff they do there?'

Three members of his audience said they had and that he was talking nonsense.

'You haven't seen anything,' insisted Arthur. 'Oh yes,' he added, because someone was offering to buy another round.

'The evidence,' he said, pointing at himself, and not missing by more than a couple of inches, 'is before your eyes. Fourteen hours in a trance,' he said, 'in a tank. In a trance. I was in a tank. I think,' he added after a thoughtful pause, 'I already said that.'

He waited patiently while the next round was duly distributed. He composed the next bit of his story in his mind, which was going to be something about the tank needing to be orientated along a line dropped perpendicularly from the Pole Star to a baseline drawn between Mars and Venus, and was about to start trying to say it when he decided to give it a miss.

'Long time,' he said instead, 'in a tank. In a trance.' He looked round severely at his audience, to make sure it was all following attentively.

He resumed.

'Where was I?' he said.

'In a trance,' said one.

'In a tank,' said another.

'Oh yes,' said Arthur. 'Thank you. And slowly,' he said, pressing onwards, 'slowly, slowly slowly, all your excess body fat turns . . . to . . .' he paused for effect, 'subcoo . . . subyoo . . . subtoocay . . .' – he paused for breath – 'subcutaneous gold, which you can have surgically removed. Getting out of the tank is hell. What did you say?'

'I was just clearing my throat.'

'I think you doubt me.'

'I was clearing my throat.'

'She was clearing her throat,' confirmed a significant part of the audience in a low rumble.

'Oh yes,' said Arthur, 'all right. And you then split the proceeds . . .' he paused again for a maths break, 'fifty-fifty with the alchemist. Make a lot of money!'

He looked swayingly around at his audience, and could not help but be aware of an air of scepticism about their jumbled faces.

He felt very affronted by this.

'How else,' he demanded, 'could I afford to have my face dropped?'

Friendly arms began to help him home. 'Listen,' he protested, as the cold February breeze brushed his face, 'looking lived-in is all the rage in California at the moment. You've got to look as if you've seen the Galaxy. Life, I mean. You've got to look as if you've seen life. That's what I got. A face drop. Give me eight years, I said. I hope being thirty doesn't come back into fashion or I've wasted a lot of money.'

He lapsed into silence for a while as the friendly arms continued to help him along the lane to his house.

'Got in yesterday,' he mumbled. 'I'm very very very happy to be home. Or somewhere very like it . . .'

'Jet lag,' muttered one of his friends. 'Long trip from California. Really mucks you up for a couple of days.'

'I don't think he's been there at all,' muttered another. 'I wonder where he *has* been. And what's happened to him.'

*

After a little sleep Arthur got up and pottered round the house a bit. He felt woozy and a little low, still disoriented by the journey. He wondered how he was going to find Fenny.

He sat and looked at the fish bowl. He tapped it again, and despite being full of water and a small yellow Babel fish which was gulping its way around rather dejectedly, it still chimed its deep and resonant chime as clearly and mesmerically as before.

Someone is trying to thank me, he thought to himself. He wondered who, and for what.

10

'At the third stroke it will be one . . . thirty-two . . . and twenty seconds.

'Beep . . . beep . . . beep.'

Ford Prefect suppressed a little giggle of evil satisfaction, realized that he had no reason to suppress it, and laughed out loud, a wicked laugh.

He switched the incoming signal through from the Sub-Etha Net to the ship's superb hi-fi system, and the odd, rather stilted, sing-song voice spoke out with remarkable clarity round the cabin.

'At the third stroke it will be one . . . thirty-two . . . and thirty seconds.

'Beep . . . beep . . . beep.'

He tweaked the volume up just a little, while keeping a careful eye on a rapidly changing table of figures on the ship's computer display. For the length of time he had in mind, the question of power consumption became significant. He didn't want a murder on his conscience.

At the third stroke it will be one ... thirty-two ... and forty seconds.

'Beep ... beep ... beep.'

He checked around the small ship. He walked down the short corridor.

'At the third stroke ...'

He stuck his head into the small, functional, gleaming steel bathroom.

'it will be ...'

It sounded fine in there.

He looked into the tiny sleeping quarters.

'... one ... thirty-two ...'

It sounded a bit muffled. There was a towel hanging over one of the speakers. He took down the towel.

'... and fifty seconds.'

Fine.

He checked out the packed cargo hold, and wasn't at all satisfied with the sound. There was altogether too much crated junk in the way. He stepped back out and waited for the door to seal. He broke open a closed control panel and pushed the jettison button. He didn't know why he hadn't thought of that before. A whooshing rumbling noise died away quickly into silence. After a pause a slight hiss could be heard again.

It stopped.

'He waited for the green light to show and then opened the door again on to the now empty cargo hold.

'... one ... thirty-three ... and fifty seconds.'

Very nice.

'Beep ... beep ... beep.'

He then went and had a last thorough examination of the emergency suspended animation chamber, which was where he particularly wanted it to be heard.

'At the third stroke it will be one ... thirty ... four ... precisely.'

He shivered as he peered down through the heavily frosted covering at the dim bulk of the form within. One day, who knew when, it would wake, and when it did, it would know what time it was. Not exactly local time, true, but what the heck.

He double-checked the computer display above the freezer bed, dimmed the lights and checked it again.

'At the third stroke it will be . . .'

He tiptoed out and resumed to the control cabin.

'. . . one . . . thirty-four and twenty seconds.'

The voice sounded as clear as if he was hearing it over a phone in London, which he wasn't, not by a long way.

He gazed out into the inky night. The star the size of a brilliant biscuit crumb he could see in the distance was Zondostina, or as it was known on the world from which the rather stilted, sing-song voice was being received, Pleiades Zeta.

The bright orange curve that filled over half the visible area was the giant gas planet Sesefras Magna, where the Xaxisian battleships docked, and just rising over its horizon was a small cool blue moon, Epun.

'At the third stroke it will be . . .'

For twenty minutes he sat and watched as the gap between the ship and Epun closed, as the ship's computer teased and kneaded the numbers that would bring it into a loop around the little moon, close the loop and keep it there, orbiting in perpetual obscurity.

'One . . . fifty-nine . . .'

His original plan had been to close down all external signalling and radiation from the ship, to render it as nearly invisible as possible unless you were actually looking at it, but then he'd had an idea he preferred. It would now emit one single continuous beam, pencil-thin, broadcasting the incoming time signal to the planet of the signal's origin, which it would not reach for four hundred years, travelling at light speed, but where it would probably cause something of a stir when it did.

'Beep . . . beep . . . beep . . .'

He sniggered.

He didn't like to think of himself as the sort of person who giggled or sniggered, but he had to admit that he had been giggling and sniggering almost continuously for well over half an hour now.

'At the third stroke . . .'

The ship was now locked almost perfectly into its perpetual orbit round a little known and never visited moon. Almost perfect.

One thing only remained. He ran again the computer simulation of the launching of the ship's little Escape-O-Buggy, balancing actions, reactions, tangential forces, all the mathematical poetry of motion, and saw that it was good.

Before he left, he turned out the lights.

As his tiny little cigar tube of an escape craft zipped out on the beginning of its three-day journey to the orbiting space station Port Sesefron, it rode for a few seconds a long pencil-thin beam of radiation that was starting out on a longer journey still.

'At the third stroke, it will be two . . . thirteen . . . and fifty seconds.'

He giggled and sniggered. He would have laughed out loud but he didn't have room.

'Beep . . . beep . . . beep.'

11

'April showers I hate especially.'

However noncommittally Arthur grunted, the man seemed determined to talk to him. He wondered if he should get up and move to another table, but there didn't seem to be one free in the whole cafeteria. He stirred his coffee fiercely.

'Bloody April showers. Hate hate hate.'

Arthur stared, frowning, out of the window. A light, sunny spray of rain hung over the motorway. Two months he'd been back now. Slipping back into his old life had in fact been laughably easy. People had such extraordinarily short memories, including him. Eight years of crazed wanderings round the Galaxy now seemed to him not so much like a bad dream as like a film he had videotaped from the TV and now kept in the back of a cupboard without bothering to watch.

One effect that still lingered, though, was his joy at being back. Now that the Earth's atmosphere had closed over his head for good, he thought, wrongly, everything within it gave him extraordinary pleasure. Looking at the silvery sparkle of the raindrops he felt he had to protest.

'Well, I like them,' he said suddenly, 'and for all the obvious reasons. They're light and refreshing. They sparkle and make you feel good.'

The man snorted derisively.

'That's what they all say,' he said, and glowered darkly from his corner seat.

He was a lorry driver. Arthur knew this because his opening, unprovoked remark had been, 'I'm a lorry driver. I hate driving in the rain. Ironic, isn't it? Bloody ironic.'

If there was a sequitur hidden in this remark, Arthur had not been able to divine it and had merely given a little grunt, affable but not encouraging.

But the man had not been deterred then, and was not deterred now. 'They all say that about bloody April showers,' he said. 'So bloody nice, so bloody refreshing, such charming bloody weather.'

He leaned forward, screwing his face up as if he was going to say something extraordinary about the government.

'What I want to know is this,' he said, 'if it's going to be nice weather, *why*,' he almost spat, 'can't it be nice without bloody raining?'

Arthur gave up. He decided to leave his coffee, which was too hot to drink quickly and too nasty to drink cold.

'Well, there you go,' he said and instead got up himself. 'Bye.'

He stopped off at the service station shop, then walked back through the car park, making a point of enjoying the fine play of rain on his face. There was even, he noticed, a hint rainbow glistening over the Devon hills. He enjoyed that too.

He climbed into his battered but adored old black Golf GTi, squealed the tyres, and headed out past the islands of petrol pumps and on to the slip road back towards the motorway.

He was wrong in thinking that the atmosphere of the Earth had closed finally and for ever above his head.

He was wrong to think that it would ever be possible to put behind him the tangled web of irresolutions into which his galactic travels had dragged him.

He was wrong to think he could now forget that the big, hard, oily, dirty, rainbow-hung Earth on which he lived was a microscopic dot on a microscopic dot lost in the unimaginable infinity of the Universe.

He drove on, humming, being wrong about all these things.

The reason he was wrong was standing by the slip road under a small umbrella.

His jaw sagged. He sprained his ankle against the brake pedal and skidded so hard he very nearly turned the car over.

'Fenny!' he shouted.

Having narrowly avoided hitting her with the actual car, he hit her instead with the car door as he leant across and flung it open at her.

It caught her hand and knocked away her umbrella, which then bowled wildly away across the road.

'Shit!' yelled Arthur as helpfully as he could, leapt out of his own door, narrowly avoided being run down by McKenna's All-Weather Haulage, and watched in horror as it ran down Fenny's umbrella instead. The lorry swept along the motorway and away.

The umbrella lay like a recently swatted daddy-long-legs, expiring sadly on the ground. Tiny gusts of wind made it twitch a little.

He picked it up.

'Er,' he said. There didn't seem to be a lot of point in offering the thing back to her.

'How did you know my name?' she said.

'Er, well,' he said. 'Look, I'll get you another one . . .'

He looked at her and tailed off.

She was tallish with dark hair which fell in waves around a pale and serious face. Standing still, alone, she seemed almost sombre, like a statue to some important but unpopular virtue in a formal garden. She seemed to be looking at something other than what she looked as if she was looking at.

But when she smiled, as she did now, it was as if she suddenly arrived from somewhere. Warmth and life flooded into her face, and impossibly graceful movement into her body. The effect was very disconcerting, and it disconcerted Arthur like hell.

She grinned, tossed her bag into the back and swivelled herself into the front seat.

'Don't worry about the umbrella,' she said to him as she climbed in. 'It was my brother's and he can't have liked it or he wouldn't have given it to me.' She laughed and pulled on her seatbelt. 'You're not a friend of my brother's, are you?'

'No.'

Her voice was the only part of her which didn't say 'Good'.

Her physical presence there in the car, his car, was quite extraordinary to Arthur. He felt, as he let the car pull slowly away, that he could hardly think or breathe, and hoped that neither of these functions were vital to his driving or they were in trouble.

So what he had experienced in the other car, her brother's car, the night he had returned exhausted and bewildered from his nightmare years in the stars, had not been the unbalance of the moment, or, if it had been, he was at least twice as unbalanced now, and quite liable to fall off whatever it is that well-balanced people are supposed to be balancing on.

'So . . .' he said, hoping to kick the conversation off to an exciting start.

'He was meant to pick me up – my brother – but phoned to say he couldn't make it. I asked about buses but the man started to look at a calendar rather than a timetable, so I decided to hitch. So.'

'So.'

'So here I am. And what I would like to know, is how you know my name.'

'Perhaps we ought to first sort out,' said Arthur, looking back over his shoulder as he eased his car into the motorway traffic, 'where I'm taking you.'

Very close, he hoped, or a long way. Close would mean she lived near him, a long way would mean he could drive her there.

'I'd like to go to Taunton,' she said, 'please. If that's all right. It's not far. You can drop me at . . .'

'You live in *Taunton*?' he said, hoping that he'd managed to sound merely curious rather than ecstatic. Taunton was wonderfully close to him. He could . . .

'No, London,' she said. 'There's a train in just under an hour.'

It was the worst thing possible. Taunton was only minutes away up the motorway. He wondered what to do, and while he was wondering with horror heard himself saying, 'Oh, I can take you to London. Let me take you to London . . .'

Bungling idiot. Why on earth had he said 'let' in that stupid way? He was behaving like a twelve-year-old.

'Are you going to London?' she asked.

'I wasn't,' he said, 'but . . .' Bungling idiot.

'It's very kind of you,' she said, 'but really no. I like to go by train.' And suddenly she was gone. Or rather, that part of her which brought her to life was gone. She looked rather distantly out of the window and hummed lightly to herself.

He couldn't believe it.

Thirty seconds into the conversation, and already he'd blown it.

Grown men, he told himself, in flat contradiction of

centuries of accumulated evidence about the way grown men behave, do not behave like this.

Taunton 5 miles, said the signpost.

He gripped the steering-wheel so tightly the car wobbled. He was going to have to do something dramatic.

'Fenny,' he said.

She glanced round sharply at him.

'You still haven't told me how . . .'

'Listen,' said Arthur, 'I will tell you, though the story is rather strange. Very strange.'

She was still looking at him, but said nothing.

'Listen . . .'

'You said that.'

'Did I? Oh. There are things I must talk to you about, and things I must tell you . . . a story I must tell you which would . . .' He was thrashing about. He wanted something along the lines of 'Thy knotted and combined locks to part, and each particular hair to stand on end like quills upon the fretful porpentine' but didn't think he could carry it off and didn't like the hedgehog reference.

'. . . which would take more than five miles,' he settled for in the end, rather lamely he was afraid.

'Well . . .'

'Just supposing,' he said, 'just supposing' – he didn't know what was coming next, so he thought he'd just sit back and listen – 'that there was some extraordinary way in which you were very important to me, and that, though you didn't know it, I was very important to you, but it all went for nothing because we only had five miles and I was a stupid idiot at knowing how to say something very important to someone I've only just met and not crash into lorries at the same time, what would you say . . .' he paused helplessly, and looked at her, 'I . . . should do?'

'Watch the road!' she yelped.

'Shit!'

He narrowly avoided careering into the side of a hundred Italian washing machines in a German lorry.

'I think,' she said, with a momentary sigh of relief, 'you should buy me a drink before my train goes.'

12

There is, for some reason, something especially grim about pubs near stations, a very particular kind of grubbiness, a special kind of pallor to the pork pies.

Worse than the pork pies, though, are the sandwiches.

There is a feeling which persists in England that making a sandwich interesting, attractive, or in any way pleasant to eat is something sinful that only foreigners do.

'Make 'em dry,' is the instruction buried somewhere in the collective national consciousness, 'make 'em rubbery. If you have to keep the buggers fresh, do it by washing 'em once a week.'

It is by eating sandwiches in pubs on Saturday lunchtimes that the British seek to atone for whatever their national sins have been. They're not altogether clear what those sins are, and don't want to know either. Sins are not the sort of things one wants to know about. But whatever sins there are are amply atoned for by the sandwiches they make themselves eat.

If there is anything worse than the sandwiches, it is the sausages which sit next to them. Joyless tubes, full of gristle, floating in a sea of something hot and sad, stuck with a plastic pin in the shape of a chef's hat: a memorial, one feels, for some chef who hated the world, and died, forgotten and alone, among his cats on a back stair in Stepney.

The sausages are for the ones who know what their sins are and wish to atone for something specific.

'There must be somewhere better,' said Arthur.

'No time,' said Fenny, glancing at her watch. 'My train leaves in half an hour.'

They sat at a small wobbly table. On it were some dirty glasses, and some soggy beermats with jokes printed on them. Arthur got Fenny a tomato juice, and himself a pint of yellow water with gas in it. And a couple of sausages. He didn't know why. He bought them for something to do while the gas settled in his glass.

The barman dunked Arthur's change in a pool of beer on the bar, for which Arthur thanked him.

'All right,' said Fenny, glancing at her watch, 'tell me what it is you have to tell me.'

She sounded, as well she might, extremely sceptical, and Arthur's heart sank. Hardly, he felt, the most conducive setting to try to explain to her as she sat there, suddenly cool and defensive, that in a sort of out-of-body dream he had had a telepathic sense that the mental breakdown she had suffered had been connected with the fact that, appearances to the contrary notwithstanding, the Earth had been demolished to make way for a new hyperspace bypass, something which he alone on Earth knew anything about, having virtually witnessed it from a Vogon spaceship, and that furthermore both his body and soul ached for her unbearably and he needed to go to bed with her as soon as was humanly possible.

'Fenny,' he started.

'I wonder if you'd like to buy some tickets for our raffle? It's just a little one.'

He glanced up sharply.

'To raise money for Anjie who's retiring.'

'What?'

'And needs a kidney machine.'

He was being leant over by a rather stiffly slim middle-aged woman with a prim knitted suit and a prim little perm, and a prim little smile that probably got licked by prim little dogs a lot.

She was holding out a small book of cloakroom tickets and a collecting tin.

'Only ten pence each,' she said, 'so you could probably even buy two. Without breaking the bank!' She gave a tinkly little laugh and then a curiously long sigh. Saying 'Without breaking the bank' had obviously given her more pleasure than anything since some GIs had been billeted on her in the war.

'Er, yes, all right,' said Arthur, hurriedly digging in his pocket and producing a couple of coins.

With infuriating slowness, and prim theatricality, if there was such a thing, the woman tore off two tickets and handed them to Arthur.

'I *do* hope you win,' she said with a smile that suddenly snapped together like a piece of advanced origami, 'the prizes are so nice.'

'Yes, thank you,' said Arthur, pocketing the tickets rather brusquely and glancing at his watch.

He turned towards Fenny.

So did the woman with the raffle tickets.

'And what about you, young lady?' she said. 'It's for Anjie's kidney machine. She's retiring, you see. Yes?'

She hoisted the little smile even further up her face. She would have to stop and let it go soon or the skin would surely split.

'Er, look, here you are,' said Arthur, and pushed a fifty pence piece at her in the hope that that would see her off.

'Oh, we *are* in the money, aren't we?' said the woman, with a long smiling sigh. 'Down from London, are we?'

Arthur wished she wouldn't talk so bloody slowly.

'No, that's all right, really,' he said with a wave of his hand, and she started with an awful deliberation to peel off five tickets, one by one.

'Oh, but you *must* have your tickets,' insisted the woman, 'or you won't be able to claim your prize. They're very nice prizes, you know. Very *suit*able.'

Arthur snatched the tickets, and said thank you as sharply as he could.

The woman turned to Fenny once again.

'And now, what about . . .'

'No!' Arthur nearly yelled. 'These are for her,' he explained, brandishing the five new tickets.

'Oh, I see! How nice!'

She smiled sickeningly at both of them.

'Well, I *do* hope you . . .'

'Yes,' snapped Arthur, 'thank you.'

The woman finally departed to the table next to theirs. Arthur turned desperately to Fenny, and was relieved to see that she was rocking with silent laughter.

He sighed and smiled.

'Where were we?'

'You were calling me Fenny, and I was about to ask you not to.'

'What do you mean?'

She twirled the little wooden cocktail stick in her tomato juice.

'It's why I asked if you were a friend of my brother's. Or half-brother, really. He's the only one who calls me Fenny, and I'm not fond of him for it.'

'So what's . . .?'

'Fenchurch.'

'What?'

'Fenchurch.'

'Fenchurch.'

She looked at him sternly.

'Yes,' she said, 'and I'm watching you like a lynx to see if you're going to ask the same silly question that everyone asks me till I want to scream. I shall be cross and disappointed if you do. Plus I shall scream. So watch it.'

She smiled, shook her hair a little forward over her face and peered at him from behind it.

'Oh,' he said, 'that's a little unfair, isn't it?'

'Yes.'

'Fine.'

'All right,' she said with a laugh, 'you can ask me. Might as well get it over with. Better than have you call me Fenny all the time.'

'Presumably . . .' said Arthur.

'We've only got *two* tickets left, you see, and since you were *so* generous when I spoke to you before . . .'

'What?' snapped Arthur.

The woman with the perm and the smile and the now nearly empty book of cloakroom tickets was now waving the two last ones under his nose.

'I thought I'd give the opportunity to you, because the prizes are so nice.'

She wrinkled up her nose a little confidentially.

'Very tasteful. I know you'll like them. And it is for Anjie's retirement present, you see. We want to give her . . .'

'A kidney machine, yes,' said Arthur. 'Here.'

He held out two more ten-pence pieces to her, and took the tickets.

A thought seemed to strike the woman. It struck her very slowly. You could watch it coming in like a long wave on a sandy beach.

'Oh dear,' she said, 'I'm not interrupting anything, am I?'

She peered anxiously at both of them.

'No, it's fine,' said Arthur. 'Everything that could possibly be fine,' he insisted, 'is fine.'

'Thank you,' he added.

'I say,' she said, in a delighted ecstacy of worry, 'you're not . . . in *love*, are you?'

'It's very hard to say,' said Arthur. 'We haven't had a chance to talk yet.'

He glanced at Fenchurch. She was grinning.

The woman nodded with knowing confidentiality.

'I'll let you see the prizes in a minute,' she said, and left.

Arthur turned, with a sigh, back to the girl that he found it hard to say whether he was in love with.

'You were about to ask me,' she said, 'a question.'

'Yes,' said Arthur.

'We can do it together if you like,' said Fenchurch. 'Was I found . . .'

'. . . in a handbag . . .' joined in Arthur.

'. . . in the Left Luggage Office . . .' they said together.

'. . . at Fenchurch Street Station,' they finished.

'And the answer,' said Fenchurch, 'is no.'

'Fine,' said Arthur.

'I was conceived there.'

'What?'

'I was con—'

'In the Left Luggage Office?' hooted Arthur.

'No, of course not. Don't be silly. What would my parents be doing in the Left Luggage Office?' she said, rather taken aback by the suggestion.

'Well, I don't know,' spluttered Arthur, 'or rather . . .'

'It was in the ticket queue.'

'The . . .'

'The ticket queue. Or so they claim. They refuse to elaborate. They only say you wouldn't believe how bored it is possible to get in the ticket queue at Fenchurch Street Station.'

She sipped demurely at her tomato juice and looked at her watch.

Arthur continued to gurgle for a moment or two.

'I'm going to have to go in a minute or two,' said Fenchurch, 'and you haven't begun to tell me whatever this terrifically extraordinary thing is that you were so keen to get off your chest.'

'Why don't you let me drive you to London?' said Arthur. 'It's Saturday, I've got nothing particular to do, I'd . . .'

'No,' said Fenchurch, 'thank you, it's sweet of you, but no. I need to be by myself for a couple of days.' She smiled and shrugged.

'But . . .'

'You can tell me another time. I'll give you my number.'

Arthur's heart went boom boom churn churn as she scribbled seven figures in pencil on a scrap of paper and handed it to him.

'Now we can relax,' she said with a slow smile which filled Arthur till he thought he would burst.

'Fenchurch,' he said, enjoying the name as he said it. 'I—'

'A box,' said a trailing voice, 'of cherry brandy liqueurs, and also, and I know you'll like this, a gramophone record of Scottish bagpipe music . . .'

'Yes, thank you, very nice,' insisted Arthur.

'I just thought I'd let you have a look at them,' said the permed woman, 'as you're down from London . . .'

She was holding them out proudly for Arthur to see. He could see that they were indeed a box of cherry brandy liqueurs and a record of bagpipe music. That was what they were.

'I'll let you have your drink in peace now,' she said, patting Arthur lightly on his seething shoulder, 'but I knew you'd like to see.'

Arthur re-engaged his eyes with Fenchurch's once again, and suddenly was at a loss for something to say. A moment had come and gone between the two of them, but the whole rhythm of it had been wrecked by that stupid, blasted woman.

'Don't worry,' said Fenchurch, looking at him steadily from over the top of her glass, 'we will talk again.' She took a sip.

'Perhaps,' she added, 'it wouldn't have gone so well if it wasn't for her.' She gave a wry smile and dropped her hair forward over her face again.

It was perfectly true.

He had to admit it was perfectly true.

13

That night, at home, as he was prancing round the house pretending to be tripping through cornfields in slow motion and continually exploding with sudden laughter, Arthur thought he could even bear to listen to the album of bagpipe music he had won. It was eight o'clock and he decided he would make himself, force himself, to listen to the whole record before he phoned her. Maybe he should even leave it till tomorrow. That would be the cool thing to do. Or next week sometime.

No. No games. He wanted her and didn't care who knew it. He definitely and absolutely wanted her, adored her, longed for her, wanted to do more things than there were names for with her.

He actually caught himself saying things like 'Yippee' as he pranced ridiculously round the house. Her eyes, her hair, her voice, everything . . .

He stopped.

He would put on the record of bagpipe music. Then he would call her.

Would he, perhaps, call her first?

No. What he would do was this. He would put on the record of bagpipe music. He would listen to it, every last banshee wail of it. Then he would call her. That was the correct order. That was what he would do.

He was worried about touching things in case they blew up when he did so.

He picked up the record. It failed to blow up. He slipped it out of its cover. He opened the record player, he turned on the amp. They both survived. He giggled foolishly as he lowered the stylus on to the disc.

He sat and listened solemnly to 'A Scottish Soldier'.

He listened to 'Amazing Grace'.

He listened to something about some glen or other.

He thought about his miraculous lunchtime.

They had just been on the point of leaving, when they were distracted by an awful outbreak of 'yoo-hooing'. The appallingly permed woman was waving to them across the room like some stupid bird with a broken wing. Everyone in the pub turned to them and seemed to be expecting some sort of response.

They hadn't listened to the bit about how pleased and happy Anjie was going to be about the £4.30p everyone had helped to raise towards the cost of her kidney machine, had been vaguely aware that someone from the next table had won a box of cherry brandy liqueurs, and took a moment or two to cotton on to the fact that the yoo-hooing lady was trying to ask them if they had ticket number 37.

Arthur discovered that he had. He glanced angrily at his watch.

Fenchurch gave him a push.

'Go on,' she said, 'go and get it. Don't be bad-tempered. Give them a nice speech about how pleased you are and you can give me a call and tell me how it went. I'll want to hear the record. Go on.'

She flicked his arm and left.

The regulars thought his acceptance speech a little over-effusive. It was, after all, merely an album of bagpipe music.

Arthur thought about it, and listened to the music, and kept on breaking into laughter.

14

Ring ring.

Ring ring.

Ring ring.

'Hello, yes? Yes, that's right. Yes. You'll 'ave to speak up, there's an awful lot of noise in 'ere. What?

'No, I only do the bar in the evenings. It's Yvonne

who does lunch, and Jim, he's the landlord. No, I wasn't on. What?

'You'll have to speak up.

'What? No, don't know anything about no raffle. What?

'No, don't know nothing about it. 'Old on! I'll call Jim.'

The barmaid put her hand over the receiver and called over the noisy bar.

''Ere, Jim, bloke on the phone says something about he's won a raffle. He keeps on saying it's ticket 37 and he's won.'

'No, there was a guy in the pub here won,' shouted back the barman.

'He says 'ave we got the ticket.'

'Well how can he think he's won if he hasn't even got a ticket?'

'Jim says 'ow can you think you've won if you 'aven't even got the ticket. What?'

She put her hand over the receiver again.

'Jim, 'e keeps effing and blinding at me. Says there's a number on the ticket.'

'Course there was a number on the ticket, it was a bloody raffle ticket, wasn't it?'

''E says 'e means it's a telephone number on the ticket.'

'Put the phone down and serve the bloody customers, will you?'

15

Eight hours west sat a man alone on a beach mourning an inexplicable loss. He could only think of his loss in little packets of grief at a time, because the whole thing was too great to be borne.

He watched the long slow Pacific waves come in along the sand, and waited and waited for the nothing that he knew was about to happen. As the time came for it not to happen, it duly didn't happen and so the afternoon wore itself away and the sun dropped beneath the long line of the sea, and the day was gone.

The beach was a beach we shall not name, because his private house was there, but it was a small sandy stretch somewhere along the hundreds of miles of coastline that first runs west from Los Angeles, which is described in the new edition of *The Hitchhiker's Guide to the Galaxy* in one entry as 'junky, wunky, lunky, stunky, and what's that other word, and all kinds of bad stuff, woo', and in another, written only hours later, as 'being like several thousand square miles of American Express junk mail, but without the same sense of moral depth. Plus the air is, for some reason, yellow.'

The coastline runs west, and then turns north up to the misty bay of San Francisco, which the *Guide* describes as a 'good place to go. It's very easy to believe that everyone you meet there also is a space traveller. Starting a new religion for you is just their way of saying "hi". Until you've settled in and got the hang of the place it is best to say "no" to three questions out of any given four that anyone may ask you, because there are some very strange things going on there, some of which an unsuspecting alien could die of.' The hundreds of curling miles of cliffs and sand, palm trees, breakers and sunsets are described in the *Guide* as 'Boffo. A good one.'

And somewhere on this good boffo stretch of coastline lay the house of this inconsolable man, a man whom many regarded as being insane. But this was only, as he would tell people, because he was.

One of the many many reasons why people thought him insane was because of the peculiarity of his house which, even in a land where most people's houses were peculiar in one way or another, was quite extreme in its peculiarness.

His house was called The Outside of the Asylum.

His name was simply John Watson, though he preferred to be called – and some of his friends had now reluctantly agreed to do this – Wonko the Sane.

In his house were a number of strange things, including a grey glass bowl with eight words engraved upon it.

We can talk of him much later on – this is just an interlude to watch the sun go down and to say that he was there watching it.

He had lost everything he cared for, and was now simply waiting for the end of the world – little realizing that it had already been and gone.

16

After a disgusting Sunday spent emptying rubbish bins behind a pub in Taunton, and finding nothing, no raffle ticket, no telephone number, Arthur tried everything he could to find Fenchurch, and the more things he tried, the more weeks passed.

He raged and railed against himself, against fate, against the world and its weather. He even, in his sorrow and his fury, went and sat in the motorway service station cafeteria where he'd been just before he met her.

'It's the drizzle that makes me particularly morose.'

'Please shut up about the drizzle,' snapped Arthur.

'I would shut up if it would shut up drizzling.'

'Look . . .'

'But I'll tell you what it will do when it shuts up drizzling, shall I?'

'No.'

'Blatter.'

'What?'

'It will blatter.'

Arthur stared over the rim of his coffee cup at the grisly outside world. It was a completely pointless place to be, he realized, and he had been driven there by superstition rather than logic. However, as if to bait him with the knowledge that such coincidences could in fact happen, fate had chosen to reunite him with the lorry driver he had encountered there last time.

The more he tried to ignore him, the more he found himself being dragged back into the gravitic whirlpool of the man's exasperating conversation.

'I think,' said Arthur vaguely, cursing himself for even bothering to say this, 'that it's easing off.'

'Ha!'

Arthur just shrugged. He should go. That's what he should do. He should just go.

'It *never* stops raining!' ranted the lorry driver. He thumped the table, spilt his tea, and actually, for a moment, appeared to be steaming.

You can't just walk off without responding to a remark like that.

'Of course it stops raining,' said Arthur. It was hardly an elegant refutation, but it had to be said.

'It *rains* . . . *all* . . . the *time*,' raved the man, thumping the table again, in time to the words.

Arthur shook his head.

'Stupid to say it rains *all* the time . . .' he said.

The man's eyebrows shot up, affronted.

'*Stupid*? Why's it stupid? Why's it stupid to say it rains all the time if it rains the whole time?'

'Didn't rain yesterday.'

'Did in Darlington.'

Arthur paused, warily.

'You going to ask me where I was yesterday?' asked the man. 'Eh?'

'No,' said Arthur.

'But I expect you can guess.'

'Do you.'

'Begins with a D.'

'Does it.'

'And it was pissing down there, I can tell you.'

'You don't want to sit there, mate,' said a passing stranger in overalls to Arthur cheerily. 'That's Thundercloud Corner, that is. Reserved special for old Raindrops Keep Falling On My Head here. There's one reserved in every motorway caff between here and sunny Denmark. Steer clear, is my advice. 'S what we all do. How's it going, Rob? Keeping busy? Got your wet-weather tyres on? Har har.'

He breezed by and went to tell a joke about Britt Ekland to someone at a nearby table.

'See, none of them bastards take me seriously,' said Rob McKenna. 'But,' he added darkly, leaning forward and screwing up his eyes, 'they all know it's true!'

Arthur frowned.

'Like my wife,' hissed the sole owner and driver of McKenna's All-Weather Haulage. 'She says it's nonsense and I make a fuss and complain about nothing, *but,*' he paused dramatically and darted out dangerous looks from his eyes, 'she always brings the washing in when I phone to say I'm on me way home!' He brandished his coffee spoon. 'What do you make of that?'

'Well . . .'

'I have a book,' he went on, 'I have a book. A diary. Kept it for fifteen years. Shows every single place I've ever been. Every day. And also what the weather was like. And it was uniformly,' he snarled, ''orrible. All over England, Scotland, Wales I been. All round the Continent, Italy, Germany, back and forth to Denmark, been to Yugoslavia. It's all marked in and charted. Even when I went to visit my brother,' he added, 'in Seattle.'

'Well,' said Arthur, getting up to leave at last, 'perhaps you'd better show it to someone.'

'I will,' said Rob McKenna.

And he did.

17

Misery. Dejection. More misery and more dejection. He needed a project and he gave himself one.

He would find where his cave had been.

On prehistoric Earth he had lived in a cave, not a nice cave, a lousy cave, but . . . There was no but. It had been a totally lousy cave and he had hated it. But he had lived in it for five years, which made it home of some kind, and a person likes to keep track of his homes. Arthur Dent was such a person and so he went to Exeter to buy a computer.

That was what he really wanted, of course, a computer. But he felt he ought to have some serious purpose in mind before he simply went and lashed out a lot of readies on what people might otherwise mistake as being just a thing to play with. So that was his serious purpose. To pinpoint the exact location of a cave on prehistoric Earth. He explained this to the man in the shop.

'Why?' said the man in the shop.

This was a tricky one.

'OK, skip that,' said the man in the shop. 'How?'

'Well, I was hoping you could help me with that.'

The man sighed and his shoulders dropped.

'Have you much experience of computers?'

Arthur wondered whether to mention Eddie the shipboard computer on the *Heart of Gold*, who could have done the job in a second, or Deep Thought, or – but decided he wouldn't.

'No,' he said.

'Looks like a fun afternoon,' said the man in the shop, but he said it only to himself.

Arthur bought the Apple anyway. Over a few days he also acquired some astronomical software, plotted the movements of stars, drew rough little diagrams of how he seemed to remember the stars to have been in the sky when he looked up out of his cave at night, and worked away busily at it for weeks, cheerfully putting off the conclusion he knew he would inevitably have to come to, which was that the whole project was completely ludicrous.

Rough drawings from memory were futile. He didn't even know how long it had been, beyond Ford Prefect's rough guess at the time that it was 'a couple of million years' and he simply didn't have the maths.

Still, in the end he worked out a method which would at least produce a result. He decided not to mind the fact that with the extraordinary jumble of rules of thumb, wild approximations and arcane guesswork he was using he would be lucky to hit the right galaxy, he just went ahead and got a result.

He would call it the right result. Who would know?

As it happened, through the myriad and unfathomable chances of fate, he got it exactly right, though he of course would never know that. He just went up to London and knocked on the appropriate door.

'Oh. I thought you were going to phone me first.'

Arthur gaped in astonishment.

'You can only come in for a few minutes,' said Fenchurch. 'I'm just going out.'

18

A summer's day in Islington, full of the mournful wail of antique-restoring machinery.

Fenchurch was unavoidably busy for the afternoon, so Arthur wandered in a blissed-out haze and looked at all the shops which, in Islington, are quite a useful bunch, as anyone who regularly needs old woodworking tools, Boer War helmets, drag, office furniture or fish will readily confirm.

The sun beat down over the roof gardens. It beat on architects and plumbers. It beat on barristers and burglars. It beat on pizzas. It beat on estate agents particulars.

It beat on Arthur as he went into a restored furniture shop.

'It's an interesting building,' said the proprietor, cheerfully. 'There's a cellar with a secret passage which connects with a nearby pub. It was built for the Prince Regent, apparently, so he could make his escape when he needed to.'

'You mean, in case anybody might catch him buying stripped pine furniture,' said Arthur.

'No,' said the proprietor, 'not for that reason.'

'You'll have to excuse me,' said Arthur. 'I'm terribly happy.'

'I see.'

He wandered hazily on and found himself outside the offices of Greenpeace. He remembered the contents of his file marked 'Things to do – urgent!', which he hadn't opened again in the meantime. He marched in with a cheery smile and said he'd come to give them some money to help free the dolphins.

'Very funny,' they told him, 'go away.'

This wasn't quite the response he had expected, so he tried again. This time they got quite angry with him, so he just left some money anyway and went back out into the sunshine.

Just after six he returned to Fenchurch's house in the alleyway, clutching a bottle of champagne.

'Hold this,' she said, shoved a stout rope in his hand and disappeared inside through the large white wooden doors from which dangled a fat padlock off a black iron bar.

The house was a small converted stable in a light industrial alleyway behind the derelict Royal Agricultural Hall of Islington. As well as its large stable doors it also had a normal-looking front door of smartly glazed panelled wood with a black dolphin door knocker. The one odd thing about this door was its doorstep, which was nine feet high, since the door was set into the upper of the two floors and presumably had been originally used to haul in hay for hungry horses.

An old pulley jutted out of the brickwork above the doorway and it was over this that the rope Arthur was holding was slung. The other end of the rope held a suspended 'cello.

The door opened above his head.

'OK,' said Fenchurch, 'pull on the rope, steady the 'cello. Pass it up to me.'

He pulled on the rope, he steadied the 'cello.

'I can't pull on the rope again,' he said, 'without letting go of the 'cello.'

Fenchurch leant down.

'I'm steadying the 'cello,' she said. 'You pull on the rope.'

The 'cello eased up level with the doorway, swinging slightly, and Fenchurch manoeuvred it inside.

'Come on up yourself,' she called down.

Arthur picked up his bag of goodies and went in through the stable doors, tingling.

The bottom room, which he had seen briefly before, was pretty rough and full of junk. A large old cast-iron mangle stood there, a surprising number of kitchen sinks were piled in a corner. There was also, Arthur was momentarily alarmed to see, a pram, but it was very old and uncomplicatedly full of books.

The floor was old stained concrete, excitingly cracked. And this was the measure of Arthur's mood as he started up the rickety wooden steps in the far corner. Even a cracked concrete floor seemed to him an almost unbearably sensual thing.

'An architect friend of mine keeps on telling me how he can do wonderful things with this place,' said Fenchurch chattily as Arthur emerged through the floor. 'He keeps on coming round, standing in stunned amazement muttering about space and objects and events and marvellous qualities of light, then says he needs a pencil and disappears for weeks. Wonderful things have, therefore, so far failed to happen to it.'

In fact, thought Arthur as he looked about, the upper room was at least reasonably wonderful anyway. It was simply decorated, furnished with things made out of cushions and also a stereo set with speakers which would have impressed the guys who put up Stonehenge.

There were flowers which were pale and pictures which were interesting.

There was a sort of gallery structure in the roof space which held a bed and also a bathroom which, Fenchurch explained, you could actually swing a cat in. 'But,' she added, 'only if it was a reasonably patient cat and didn't mind a few nasty cracks about the head. So. Here you are.'

'Yes.'

They looked at each other for a moment.

The moment became a longer moment, and suddenly it was a very long moment, so long one could hardly tell where all the time was coming from.

For Arthur, who could usually contrive to feel self-conscious if left alone for long enough with a Swiss cheese plant, the moment was one of sustained revelation. He felt on the sudden like a cramped and zoo-born animal who awakes one morning to find the door to his cage hanging quietly open and the savannah stretching grey and pink to the distant rising sun, while all around new sounds are waking.

He wondered what the new sounds were as he gazed at her openly wondering face and her eyes that smiled with a shared surprise.

He hadn't realized that life speaks with a voice to you, a voice that brings you answers to the questions you continually ask of it, had never consciously detected it or recognized its tones till it now said something it had never said to him before, which was 'Yes'.

Fenchurch dropped her eyes away at last, with a tiny shake of her head.

'I know,' she said. 'I shall have to remember,' she added, 'that you are the sort of person who cannot hold on to a simple piece of paper for two minutes without winning a raffle with it.'

She turned away.

'Let's go for a walk,' she said quickly. 'Hyde Park. I'll change into something less suitable.'

She was dressed in a rather severe dark dress, not a particularly shapely one, and it didn't really suit her.

'I wear it specially for my 'cello teacher,' she said. 'He's a nice old boy, but I sometimes think all that bowing gets him a bit excited. I'll be down in a moment.'

She ran lightly up the steps to the gallery above, and called down, 'Put the bottle in the fridge for later.'

He noticed as he slipped the champagne bottle into the door that it had an identical twin to sit next to.

He walked over to the window and looked out. He turned and started to look at her records. From above he heard the rustle of her dress fall to the ground. He talked to himself about the sort of person he was. He told himself very firmly that for this moment at least he would keep his eyes very firmly and steadfastly locked on to the spines of her records, read the titles, nod appreciatively, count the blasted things if he had to. He would keep his head down.

This he completely, utterly and abjectly failed to do.

She was staring down at him with such intensity that she seemed hardly to notice that he was looking up at her. Then suddenly she shook her head, dropped the light sundress down over herself and disappeared quickly into the bathroom.

She emerged a moment later, all smiles and with a sunhat and came tripping down the steps with extraordinary lightness. It was a strange kind of dancing motion she had. She saw that he noticed it and put her head slightly on one side.

'Like it?' she said.

'You look gorgeous,' he said simply, because she did.

'Hmmmm,' she said, as if he hadn't really answered her question.

She closed the upstairs front door, which had stood open all this time, and looked around the little room to see that it was all in a fit state to be left on its own for a while. Arthur's eyes followed hers around, and while he was looking in the other direction she slipped something out of a drawer and into the canvas bag she was carrying.

Arthur looked back at her.

'Ready?'

'Did you know,' she said with a slightly puzzled smile, 'that there's something wrong with me?'

Her directness caught Arthur unprepared.

'Well,' he said, 'I'd heard some vague sort of . . .'

'I wonder how much you do know about me,' she said. 'If you heard from where I think you heard then that's not it. Russell just sort of makes stuff up, because he can't deal with what it really is.'

A pang of worry went through Arthur.

'Then what is it?' he said. 'Can you tell me?'

'Don't worry,' she said, 'it's nothing bad at all. Just unusual. Very very unusual.'

She touched his hand, and then leant forward and kissed him briefly.

'I shall be very interested to know,' she said, 'if you manage to work out what it is this evening.'

Arthur felt that if someone tapped him at that point he would have chimed, like the deep sustained rolling chime his grey fishbowl made when he flicked it with his thumbnail.

19

Ford Prefect was irritated to be continually wakened by the sound of gunfire.

He slid himself out of the maintenance hatchway which he had fashioned into a bunk for himself by disabling some of the noisier machinery in its vicinity and padding it with towels. He slung himself down the access ladder and prowled the corridors moodily.

They were claustrophobic and ill-lit, and what light there was was continually flickering and dimming as power surged this way and that through the ship, causing heavy vibrations and rasping humming noises.

That wasn't it, though.

He paused and leaned back against the wall as something that looked like a small silver power drill flew past him down the dim corridor with a nasty searing screech.

That wasn't it either.

He clambered listlessly through a bulkhead door and found himself in a larger corridor, though still ill-lit.

The ship lurched. It had been doing this a fair bit, but this was heavier. A small platoon of robots went by making a terrible clattering.

Still not it, though.

Acrid smoke was drifting up from one end of the corridor, so he walked along it in the other direction.

He passed a series of observation monitors let into the walls behind plates of toughened but still badly scratched Perspex.

One of them showed some horrible green scaly reptilian figure ranting and raving about the Single Transferable Vote system. It was hard to tell whether he was for or against it, but he clearly felt very strongly about it. Ford turned the sound down.

That wasn't it, though.

He passed another monitor. It was showing a commercial for some brand of toothpaste that would apparently make you feel free if you used it. There was nasty blaring music with it too, but that wasn't it.

He came upon another, much larger three-dimensional screen that was monitoring the outside of the vast silver Xaxisian ship.

As he watched, a thousand horribly beweaponed Zirzla robot starcruisers came searing round the dark shadow of a moon, silhouetted against the blinding disc of the star Xaxis, and the ship simultaneously unleashed a vicious blaze of hideously incomprehensible forces from all its orifices against them.

That was it.

Ford shook his head irritably and rubbed his eyes. He slumped on the wrecked body of a dull silver robot which clearly had been burning earlier on, but had now cooled down enough to sit on.

He yawned and dug his copy of *The Hitchhiker's Guide to the Galaxy* out of his satchel. He activated the screen, and flicked idly through some level three entries and some level four entries. He was looking for some good insomnia cures. He found REST, which was what he reckoned he needed. He found REST AND RECUPERATION and was about to pass on when he suddenly had a better idea. He looked up at the monitor screen. The battle was raging more fiercely every second and the noise was appalling. The ship juddered, screamed, and lurched as each new bolt of stunning energy was delivered or received.

He looked back down at the *Guide* again and flipped through a few likely locations. He suddenly laughed, and then rummaged in his satchel again.

He pulled out a small memory dump module, wiped off the fluff and biscuit crumbs, and plugged it into an interface on the back of the *Guide*.

When all the information that he could think was relevant had been dumped into the module, he unplugged it again, tossed it lightly in the palm of his hand, put the *Guide* away in his satchel, smirked, and went in search of the ship's computer data banks.

20

'The purpose of having the sun go low in the evenings, in the summer, especially in parks,' said the voice earnestly, 'is to make girls' breasts bob up and down more clearly to the eye. I am convinced that this is the case.'

Arthur and Fenchurch giggled about this to each

other as they passed. She hugged him more tightly for a moment.

'And I am certain,' said the frizzy ginger-haired youth with the long thin nose who was expostulating from his deckchair by the side of the Serpentine, 'that if one worked the argument through, one would find that it flowed with perfect naturalness and logic from everything,' he insisted to his thin dark-haired companion who was slumped in the next door deckchair feeling dejected about his spots, 'that Darwin was going on about. This is certain. This is indisputable. And,' he added, 'I love it.'

He turned sharply and squinted through his spectacles at Fenchurch. Arthur steered her away and could feel her silently quaking.

'Next guess,' she said, when she had stopped giggling, 'come on.'

'All right,' he said, 'your elbow. Your left elbow. There's something wrong with your left elbow.'

'Wrong again,' she said, 'completely wrong. You're on completely the wrong track.'

The summer sun was sinking through the trees in the park, looking as if— Let's not mince words. Hyde Park is stunning. Everything about it is stunning except for the rubbish on Monday mornings. Even the ducks are stunning. Anyone who can go through Hyde Park on a summer's evening and not feel moved by it is probably going through in an ambulance with the sheet pulled over their face.

It is a park in which people do more extraordinary things than they do elsewhere. Arthur and Fenchurch found a man in shorts practising the bagpipes to himself under a tree. The piper paused to chase off an American couple who had tried, timidly, to put some coins on the box his bagpipes came in.

'No!' he shouted at them. 'Go away! I'm only practising.'

He started resolutely to reinflate his bag, but even the noise this made could not disfigure their mood.

Arthur put his arms around her and moved them slowly downwards.

'I don't think it can be your bottom,' he said after a while, 'there doesn't seem to be anything wrong with that at all.'

'Yes,' she agreed, 'there's absolutely nothing wrong with my bottom.'

They kissed for so long that eventually the piper went and practised on the other side of the tree.

'I'll tell you a story,' said Arthur.

'Good.'

They found a patch of grass which was relatively free of couples actually lying on top of each other and sat and watched the stunning ducks and the low sunlight rippling on the water which ran beneath the stunning ducks.

'A story,' said Fenchurch, cuddling his arm to her.

'Which will tell something of the sort of things that happen to me. It's absolutely true.

'You know sometimes people tell you stories that are supposed to be something that happened to their wife's cousin's best friend, but actually probably got made up somewhere along the line.

'Well, it's like one of those stories, except that it actually happened, and I know it actually happened, because the person it actually happened to was me.'

'Like the raffle ticket.'

Arthur laughed. 'Yes. I had a train to catch,' he went on. 'I arrived at the station—'

'Did I ever tell you,' interrupted Fenchurch, 'what happened to my parents in a station?'

'Yes,' said Arthur, 'you did.'

'Just checking.'

Arthur glanced at his watch. 'I suppose we could think of getting back,' he said.

'Tell me the story,' said Fenchurch firmly. 'You arrived at the station.'

'I was about twenty minutes early. I'd got the time of the train wrong. I suppose it is at least equally possible,' he added after a moment's reflection, 'that British Rail had got the time of the train wrong. Hadn't occurred to me before.'

'Get on with it.' Fenchurch laughed.

'So I bought a newspaper, to do the crossword, and went to the buffet to get a cup of coffee.'

'You do the crossword?'

'Yes.'

'Which one?'

'The *Guardian* usually.'

'I think it tries to be too cute. I prefer *The Times*. Did you solve it?'

'What?'

'The crossword in the *Guardian*.'

'I haven't had a chance to look at it yet,' said Arthur, 'I'm still trying to buy the coffee.'

'All right, then. Buy the coffee.'

'I'm buying it. I am also,' said Arthur, 'buying some biscuits.'

'What sort?'

'Rich Tea.'

'Good choice.'

'I like them. Laden with all these new possessions, I go and sit at a table. And don't ask me what the table was like because this was some time ago and I can't remember. It was probably round.'

'All right.'

'So let me give you the layout. Me sitting at the table. On my left, the newspaper. On my right, the cup of coffee. In the middle of the table, the packet of biscuits.'

'I see it perfectly.'

'What you don't see,' said Arthur, 'because I haven't mentioned him yet, is the guy sitting at the table already. He is sitting there opposite me.'

'What's he like?'

'Perfectly ordinary. Briefcase. Business suit. He didn't look,' said Arthur, 'as if he was about to do anything weird.'

'Ah. I know the type. What did he do?'

'He did this. He leaned across the table, picked up the packet of biscuits, tore it open, took one out, and . . .'

'What?'

'Ate it.'

'*What?*'

'He ate it.'

Fenchurch looked at him in astonishment. 'What on earth did you do?'

'Well, in the circumstances I did what any red-blooded Englishman would do. I was compelled,' said Arthur, 'to ignore it.'

'*What?* Why?'

'Well, it's not the sort of thing you're trained for, is it? I searched my soul, and discovered that there was nothing anywhere in my upbringing, experience or even primal instincts to tell me how to react to someone who has quite simply, calmly, sitting right there in front of me, stolen one of my biscuits.'

'Well, you could . . .' Fenchurch thought about it. 'I must say I'm not sure what I would have done either. So what happened?'

'I stared furiously at the crossword,' said Arthur. 'Couldn't do a single clue, took a sip of coffee, it was too hot to drink, so there was nothing for it. I braced myself. I took a biscuit, trying very hard not to notice,' he added, 'that the packet was already mysteriously open . . .'

'But you're fighting back, taking a tough line.'

'After my fashion, yes. I ate the biscuit. I ate it very deliberately and visibly, so that he would have no doubt as to what it was I was doing. When I eat a biscuit,' Arthur said, 'it stays eaten.'

'So what did he do?'

'Took another one. Honestly,' insisted Arthur, 'this is exactly what happened. He took another biscuit, he ate it. Clear as daylight. Certain as we are sitting on the ground.'

Fenchurch stirred uncomfortably.

'And the problem was,' said Arthur, 'that having not said anything the *first* time, it was somehow even more difficult to broach the subject the second time around. What do you say? "Excuse me . . . I couldn't help noticing, er . . ." Doesn't work. No, I ignored it with, if anything, even more vigour than previously.'

'My man . . .'

'Stared at the crossword, again, still couldn't budge a bit of it, so showing some of the spirit that Henry V did on St Crispin's Day . . .'

'What?'

'I went into the breach again. I took,' said Arthur, 'another biscuit. And for an instant our eyes met.'

'Like this?'

'Yes, well, no, not quite like that. But they met. Just for an instant. And we both looked away. But I am here to tell you,' said Arthur, 'that there was a little electricity in the air. There was a little tension building up over the table. At about this time.'

'I can imagine.'

'We went through the whole packet like this. Him, me, him, me . . .'

'The *whole* packet?'

'Well, it was only eight biscuits but it seemed like a lifetime of biscuits we were getting through at this point. Gladiators could hardly have had a tougher time.'

'Gladiators,' said Fenchurch, 'would have had to do it in the sun. More physically gruelling.'

'There is that. So. When the empty packet was lying dead between us the man at last got up, having done his worst, and left. I heaved a sigh of relief, of course. As it happened, my train was announced a moment or two later, so I finished my coffee, stood up, picked up the newspaper, and underneath the newspaper . . .'

'Yes?'

'Were *my* biscuits.'

'What?' said Fenchurch. '*What?*'

'True.'

'No!' She gasped and tossed herself back on the grass laughing.

She sat up again.

'You complete nitwit,' she hooted, 'you almost completely and utterly foolish person.'

She pushed him backwards, rolled over him, kissed him and rolled off again. He was surprised at how light she was.

'Now you tell me a story.'

'I thought,' she said putting on a low husky voice, 'that you were very keen to get back.'

'No hurry,' he said airily, 'I want you to tell me a story.'

She looked out over the lake and pondered.

'All right,' she said, 'it's only a short one. And not funny like yours, but . . . Anyway.'

She looked down. Arthur could feel that it was one of those sorts of moments. The air seemed to stand still around them, waiting. Arthur wished that the air would go away and mind its own business.

'When I was a kid,' she said. 'These sort of stories always start like this, don't they, "When I was a kid . . . ." Anyway. This is the bit where the girl suddenly says, "When I was a kid" and starts to unburden herself. We have got to that bit. When I was a kid I had this picture hanging over the foot of my bed . . . What do you think of it so far?'

'I like it. I think it's moving well. You're getting the bedroom interest in nice and early. We could probably do with some development with the picture.'

'It was one of those pictures that children are supposed to like,' she said, 'but don't. Full of endearing little animals doing endearing things, you know?'

'I know. I was plagued with them too. Rabbits in waistcoats.'

'Exactly. These rabbits were in fact on a raft, as were assorted rats and owls. There may even have been a reindeer.'

'On the raft.'

'On the raft. And a boy was sitting on the raft.'

'Among the rabbits in waistcoats and the owls and the reindeer.'

'Precisely there. A boy of the cheery gypsy ragamuffin variety.'

'Ugh.'

'The picture worried me, I must say. There was an otter swimming in front of the raft, and I used to lie awake at night worrying about this otter having to pull the raft, with all these wretched animals on it who shouldn't even be on a raft, and the otter had such a thin tail to pull it with I thought it must hurt pulling it all the time. Worried me. Not badly, but just vaguely, all the time.

'Then one day – and remember I'd been looking at this picture every night for years – I suddenly noticed that the raft had a sail. Never seen it before. The otter was fine, he was just swimming along.'

She shrugged.

'Good story?' she said.

'Ends weakly,' said Arthur, 'leaves the audience crying "Yes, but what of it?" Fine up till there, but needs a final sting before the credits.'

Fenchurch laughed and hugged her legs.

'It was just such a sudden revelation, years of almost unnoticed worry just dropping away, like taking off heavy weights, like black and white becoming colour, like a dry stick suddenly being watered. The sudden shift of perspective that says, "Put away your worries, the world is a good and perfect place. It is in fact very easy." You probably think I'm saying that because I'm going to say that I felt like that this afternoon or something, don't you?'

'Well, I . . .' said Arthur, his composure suddenly shattered.

'Well, it's all right,' she said, 'I did. That's exactly what I felt. But you see, I've felt that before, even stronger. Incredibly strongly. I'm afraid I'm a bit of a one,' she said, gazing off into the distance, 'for sudden startling revelations.'

Arthur was at sea, could hardly speak, and felt it wiser, therefore, for the moment not to try.

'It was very *odd*,' she said, much as one of the pursuing Egyptians might have said that the behaviour of the Red Sea when Moses waved his rod at it was a little on the strange side.

'Very odd,' she repeated, 'for days before, the strangest feeling had been building in me, as if I was going to give birth. No, it wasn't like that in fact, it was more as if I was being connected into something, bit by bit. No, not even that; it was as if the whole of the Earth, through me, was going to . . .'

'Does the number,' said Arthur gently, 'forty-two mean anything to you at all?'

'What? No, what are you talking about?' exclaimed Fenchurch.

'Just a thought,' murmured Arthur.

'Arthur, I mean this, this is very real to me, this is serious.'

'*I* was being perfectly serious,' said Arthur. 'It's just the Universe I'm never quite sure about.'

'What do you mean by that?'

'Tell me the rest of it,' he said. 'Don't worry if it sounds odd. Believe me, you are talking to someone who has seen a lot of stuff,' he added, 'that is odd. And I don't mean biscuits.'

She nodded, and seemed to believe him. Suddenly, she gripped his arm.

'It was so *simple*,' she said, 'so wonderfully and extraordinarily simple, when it came.'

'What was it?' said Arthur quietly.

'Arthur, you see,' she said, 'that's what I no longer know. And the loss is unbearable. If I try to think back to it, it all goes flickery and jumpy, and if I try too hard, I get as far as the teacup and I just black out.'

'What?'

'Well, like your story,' she said, 'the best bit happened in a café. I was sitting there, having a cup of tea. This was after days of this build up, the feeling of becoming connected up. I think I was buzzing gently. And there was some work going on at a building site opposite the café, and I was watching it through the window, over the rim of my teacup, which I always find is the nicest way of watching other people working. And suddenly, there it was in my mind, this message from somewhere. And it was so simple. It made such sense of everything. I just sat up and thought, "Oh! Oh, well that's all right, then." I was so startled I almost dropped my teacup, in fact I think I did drop it. Yes,' she added thoughtfully, 'I'm sure I did. How much sense am I making?'

'It was fine up to the bit about the teacup.'

She shook her head, and shook it again, as if trying to clear it, which is what she was trying to do.

'Well, that's it,' she said. 'Fine up to the bit about the teacup. That was the point at which it seemed to me quite literally as if the world exploded.'

'What . . .?'

'I know it sounds crazy, and everybody says it was hallucinations, but if that was hallucinations then I have hallucinations in big-screen 3D with 16-track Dolby Stereo and should probably hire myself out to people who are bored with shark movies. It was as if the ground was literally ripped from under my feet, and . . . and . . .'

She patted the grass lightly, as if for reassurance, and then seemed to change her mind about what she was going to say.

'And I woke up in hospital. I suppose I've been in and out ever since. And that's why I have an instinctive nervousness,' she said, 'of sudden startling revelations that everything's going to be all right.' She looked up at him.

Arthur had simply ceased to worry himself about the strange anomalies surrounding his return to his home world, or rather had consigned them to that part of his mind marked 'Things to think about – Urgent.' 'Here is the world,' he had told himself. 'Here, for whatever reason, is the world, and here it stays. With me on it.' But now it seemed to go swimmy around him, as it had that night in the car when Fenchurch's brother had told him the silly stories of the CIA agent in the reservoir. The French Embassy went swimmy. The trees went swimmy. The lake went swimmy, but this was perfectly natural and nothing to be alarmed by because a grey goose had just landed on it. The geese were having a great relaxed time and had no major answers they wished to know the questions to.

'Anyway,' said Fenchurch, suddenly and brightly and with a wide-eyed smile, 'there is something wrong with part of me, and you've got to find out what it is. We'll go home.'

Arthur shook his head.

'What's the matter?' she said.

Arthur had shaken his head, not to disagree with her suggestion which he thought was a truly excellent one, one of the world's great suggestions, but because he was just for a moment trying to free himself of the recurring impression he had that just when he was least expecting it the Universe would suddenly leap out from behind a door and go boo at him.

'I'm just trying to get this entirely clear in my mind,' said Arthur, 'you say you felt as if the Earth actually . . . exploded . . .'

'Yes. More than felt.'

'Which is what everybody else says,' he said hesitantly, 'is hallucinations?'

'Yes, but Arthur, that's ridiculous. People think that if you just say "hallucinations" it explains anything you want it to explain and eventually whatever it is you can't understand will just go away. It's just a word, it doesn't explain anything. It doesn't explain why the dolphins disappeared.'

'No,' said Arthur. 'No,' he added thoughtfully. 'No,' he added again, even more thoughtfully. 'What?' he said at last.

'Doesn't explain the dolphins disappearing.'

'No,' said Arthur, 'I see that. Which dolphins do you mean?'

'What do you mean which dolphins? I'm talking about when all the dolphins disappeared.'

She put her hand on his knee, which made him realize that the tingling going up and down his spine was not her gently stroking his back, and must instead be one of the nasty creepy feelings he so often got when people were trying to explain things to him.

'The dolphins?'

'Yes.'

'All the dolphins,' said Arthur, 'disappeared?'

'Yes.'

'The dolphins? You're saying the dolphins all disappeared? Is this,' said Arthur, trying to be absolutely clear on this point, 'what you're saying?'

'Arthur, where have you been, for Heaven's sake? The dolphins all disappeared on the same day I . . .'

She stared him intently in his startled eyes.

'What . . .?'

'No dolphins. All gone. Vanished.'

She searched his face.

'Did you really not know that?'

It was clear from his startled expression that he did not.

'Where did they go?' he asked.

'No one knows. That's what vanished means.' She paused. 'Well, there is one man who says he knows about it, but everyone says he lives in California,' she said, 'and is mad. I was thinking of going to see him because it seems the only lead I've got on what happened to me.'

She shrugged, and then looked at him long and quietly. She laid her hand on the side of his face.

'I really would like to know where you've been,' she said. 'I think something terrible happened to you then as well. And that's why we recognized each other.'

She glanced around the park, which was now being gathered into the clutches of dusk.

'Well,' she said, 'now you've got someone you can tell.'

Arthur slowly let out a long year of a sigh.

'It is,' he said, 'a very long story.'

Fenchurch leaned across him and drew over her canvas bag.

'Is it anything to do with this?' she said. The thing she took out of her bag was battered and travelworn as it had been hurled into prehistoric rivers, baked under the sun that shines so redly on the deserts of Kakrafoon, half-buried in the marbled sands that fringe the heady vapoured oceans of Santraginus V, frozen on the glaciers of the moon of Jaglan Beta, sat on, kicked around spaceships, scuffed and generally abused, and since its makers had thought that these were exactly the sorts of things that might happen to it, they had thoughtfully encased it in a sturdy plastic cover and written on it, in large friendly letters, the words DON'T PANIC.

'Where did you get this?' said Arthur, startled, taking it from her.

'Ah,' she said, 'I thought it was yours. In Russell's car that night. You dropped it. Have you been to many of these places?'

Arthur drew *The Hitchhiker's Guide to the Galaxy* from

its cover. It was like a small, thin, flexible lap-computer. He tapped some buttons till the screen flared with text.

'A few,' he said.

'Can we go to them?'

'What? No,' said Arthur abruptly, then relented, but relented warily. 'Do you want to?' he said, hoping for the answer no. It was an act of great generosity on his part not to say, 'You don't want to, do you?' which expects it.

'Yes,' she said. 'I want to know what the message was that I lost, and where it came from. Because I don't think,' she added, standing up and looking round the increasing gloom of the park, 'that it came from here.'

'I'm not even sure,' she further added, slipping her arm around Arthur's waist, 'that I know where here is.'

21

The Hitchhiker's Guide to the Galaxy is, as has been remarked before often and accurately, a pretty startling kind of a thing. It is, essentially, as the title implies, a guide book. The problem is, or rather one of the problems, for there are many, a sizeable proportion of which are continually clogging up the civil, commercial and criminal courts in all areas of the Galaxy, and especially, where possible, the more corrupt ones, this.

The previous sentence makes sense. That is not the problem.

This is:

Change.

Read it through again and you'll get it.

The Galaxy is a rapidly changing place. There is,

frankly, so much of it, every bit of which is continually on the move, continually changing. A bit of a nightmare, you might think, for a scrupulous and conscientious editor diligently striving to keep this massively detailed and complex electronic tome abreast of all the changing circumstances and conditions that the Galaxy throws up every minute of every hour of every day, and you would be wrong. Where you would be wrong would be in failing to realize that the editor, like all the editors the *Guide* has ever had, has no real grasp of the meanings of the words 'scrupulous', 'conscientious' or 'diligent', and tends to get his nightmares through a straw.

Entries tend to get updated or not across the Sub-Etha Net according to if they read good.

Take for example, the case of Brequinda in the Foth of Avalars, famed in myth, legend and stultifyingly dull tri-D mini-serieses as home of the magnificent and magical Fuolornis Fire Dragon.

In Ancient days, before the Advent of the Sorth of Bragadox, when Fragilis sang and Saxaquine of the Quenelux held sway, when the air was sweet and the nights fragrant, but everyone somehow managed to be, or so they claimed, though how on earth they could have thought that anyone was even remotely likely to believe such a preposterous claim what with all the sweet air and fragrant nights and whatnot is anyone's guess, virgins, it was not possible to heave a brick on Brequinda in the Foth of Avalars without hitting at least half a dozen Fuolornis Fire Dragons.

Whether you would want to do that is another matter.

Not that Fire Dragons weren't an essentially peace-loving species, because they were. They adored it to bits, and this wholesale adoring of things to bits was often in itself the problem: one so often hurts the one one loves, especially if one is a Fuolornis Fire Dragon with breath like a rocket booster and teeth like a park fence. Another problem was that once they were in the mood they often went on to hurt quite a lot of the ones that other people loved as well. Add to all that the relatively small number of madmen who actually went around the place heaving bricks, and you end up with a lot of people on Brequinda in the Foth of Avalars getting seriously hurt by dragons.

But did they mind? They did not.

Were they heard to bemoan their fate? No.

The Fuolornis Fire Dragons were revered throughout the lands of Brequinda in the Foth of Avalars for their savage beauty, their noble ways and their habit of biting people who didn't revere them.

Why was this?

The answer was simple.

Sex.

There is, for some unfathomed reason, something almost unbearably sexy about having huge fire-breathing magical dragons flying low about the sky on moonlit nights which were already dangerously on the sweet and fragrant side.

Why this should be so, the romance-besotted people of Brequinda in the Foth of Avalars could not have told you, and would not have stopped to discuss the matter once the effect was up and going, for no sooner would a flock of half a dozen silk-winged leather-bodied Fuolornis Fire Dragons heave into sight across the evening horizon than half the people of Brequinda were scurrying off into the woods with the other half, there to spend a busy breathless night together and emerge with the first rays of dawn all smiling and happy and still claiming, rather endearingly, to be virgins, if rather flushed and sticky virgins.

Pheromones, some researchers said.

Something sonic, others claimed.

The place was always stiff with researchers trying to get to the bottom of it all and taking a very long time about it.

Not surprisingly, the *Guide*'s graphically enticing description of the general state of affairs on this planet has proved to be astonishingly popular amongst hitch-hikers who allow themselves to be guided by it, and so it has simply never been taken out, and it is therefore left to latter-day travellers to find out for themselves that today's modern Brequinda in the City State of Avalars is now little more than concrete, strip joints and Dragon Burger Bars.

22

The night in Islington was sweet and fragrant.

There were, of course, no Fuolornis Fire Dragons about in the alley, but if any had chanced by they might just as well have sloped off across the road for a pizza, for they were not going to be needed.

Had an emergency cropped up while they were still in the middle of their American Hots with extra anchovy they could always have sent across a message to put Dire Straits on the stereo, which is now known to have much the same effect.

'No,' said Fenchurch, 'not yet.'

Arthur put Dire Straits on the stereo. Fenchurch pushed ajar the upstairs front door to let in a little more of the sweet fragrant night air. They both sat on some of the furniture made out of cushions, very close to the open bottle of champagne.

'No,' said Fenchurch, 'not till you've found out what's wrong with me, which bit. But I suppose,' she added, very, very, very quietly, 'that we may as well start with where your hand is now.'

Arthur said, 'So which way do I go?'

'Down,' said Fenchurch, 'on this occasion.'

He moved his hand.

'Down,' she said, 'is in fact the other way.'

'Oh yes.'

Mark Knopfler has an extraordinary ability to make a Schecter Custom Stratocaster hoot and sing like angels on a Saturday night, exhausted from being good all week and needing a stiff beer – which is not strictly relevant at this point since the record hadn't yet got to that bit, but there will be too much else going on when it does, and furthermore the chronicler does not intend to sit here with a track list and a stopwatch, so it seems best to mention it now while things are still moving slowly.

'And so we come,' said Arthur, 'to your knee. There is something terribly and tragically wrong with your left knee.'

'My left knee,' said Fenchurch, 'is absolutely fine.'

'So it is.'

'Did you know that . . .'

'What?'

'Ahm, it's all right, I can tell you do. No, keep going.'

'So it has to be something to do with your feet . . .'

She smiled in the dim light, and wriggled her shoulders noncommittally against the cushions. Since there are cushions in the Universe, on Squornshellous Beta to be exact, two worlds in from the swampland of the mattresses, that actively enjoy being wriggled against, particularly if it's noncommittally because of the syncopated way in which the shoulders move, it's a pity they weren't there. They weren't, but such is life.

Arthur held her left foot in his lap and looked it over carefully. All kinds of stuff about the way her dress fell away from her legs was making it difficult for him to think particularly clearly at this point.

'I have to admit,' he said, 'that I really don't know what I'm looking for.'

'You'll know when you find it,' she said. 'Really you will.' There was a slight catch in her voice. 'It's not that one.'

Feeling increasingly puzzled, Arthur let her left foot down on to the floor and moved himself around so that he could take her right foot. She moved forward, put her arms round and kissed him, because the record had got to that bit which, if you knew the record, you would know made it impossible not to do this.

Then she gave him her right foot.

He stroked it, ran his fingers round her ankle, under her toes, along her instep, could find nothing wrong with it.

She watched him with great amusement, laughed and shook her head.

'No, don't stop,' she said, 'but it's not that one now.'

Arthur stopped, and frowned at her left foot on the floor.

'Don't stop.'

He stroked her right foot, ran his fingers around her ankle, under her toes, along her instep and said, 'You mean it's something to do with which leg I'm holding . . .?'

She did another of the shrugs which would have brought such joy into the life of a simple cushion from Squornshellous Beta.

He frowned.

'Pick me up,' she said quietly.

He let her right foot down to the floor and stood up. So did she. He picked her up in his arms and they kissed again. This went on for a while, then she said, 'Now put me down again.'

Still puzzled, he did so.

'Well?'

She looked at him almost challengingly.

'So what's wrong with my feet?' she said.

Arthur still did not understand. He sat on the floor, then got down on his hands and knees to look at her feet, in situ, as it were, in their normal habitat. And as he looked closely, something odd struck him. He put his head right down to the ground and peered. There was a long pause. He sat back heavily.

'Yes,' he said, 'I see what's wrong with your feet. They don't touch the ground.'

'So . . . so what do you think . . .?'

Arthur looked up at her quickly and saw the deep apprehension making her eyes suddenly dark. She bit her lip and was trembling.

'What do . . .' she stammered. 'Are you . . .?' She shook the hair forwards over her eyes that were filling with dark fearful tears.

He stood up quickly, put his arms around her and gave her a single kiss.

'Perhaps you can do what I can do,' he said, and walked straight out of her upstairs front door.

The record got to the good bit.

23

The battle raged on about the star of Xaxis. Hundreds of the fierce and horribly beweaponed Zirzla ships had now been smashed and wrenched to atoms by the withering forces the huge silver Xaxisian ship was able to deploy.

Part of the moon had gone too, blasted away by those same blazing forceguns that ripped the very fabric of space as they passed through it.

The Zirzla ships that remained, horribly beweaponed though they were, were now hopelessly outclassed by the devastating power of the Xaxisian ship, and were fleeing for cover behind the rapidly disintegrating moon, when the Xaxisian ship, in hurtling pursuit behind them, suddenly announced that it needed a holiday and left the field of battle.

All was redoubled fear and consternation for a moment, but the ship was gone.

With the stupendous powers at its command it flitted across vast tracts of irrationally shaped space quickly, effortlessly, and above all, quietly.

Deep in his greasy, smelly bunk, fashioned out of a maintenance hatchway, Ford Prefect slept among his towels, dreaming of old haunts. He dreamed at one point in his slumbers of New York.

In his dream he was walking late at night along the East Side, beside the river which had become so extravagantly polluted that new lifeforms were now emerging from it spontaneously, demanding welfare and voting rights.

One of these now floated past, waving. Ford waved back.

The thing thrashed to the shore and struggled up the bank.

'Hi,' it said, 'I've just been created. I'm completely new to the Universe in all respects. Is there anything you can tell me?'

'Phew,' said Ford, a little nonplussed, 'I can tell you where some bars are, I guess.'

'What about love and happiness. I sense deep needs for things like that,' it said, waving its tentacles. 'Got any leads there?'

'You can get some like what you require,' said Ford, 'on Seventh Avenue.'

'I instinctively feel,' said the creature, urgently, 'that I need to be beautiful. Am I?'

'You're pretty direct, aren't you?'

'No point in mucking about. Am I?'

The thing was oozing all over the place now, squelching and blubbering. A nearby wino was getting interested.

'To me?' said Ford. 'No. But listen,' he added after a moment, 'most people make out, you know. Are there any like you down there?'

'Search me, buster,' said the creature, 'as I said, I'm new here. Life is entirely strange to me. What's it like?'

Here was something that Ford felt he could speak about with authority.

'Life,' he said, 'is like a grapefruit.'

'Er, how so?'

'Well, it's sort of orangey-yellow and dimpled on the outside, wet and squidgy in the middle. It's got pips inside too. Oh, and some people have half a one for breakfast.'

'Is there anyone else out there I can talk to?'

'I expect so,' said Ford. 'Ask a policeman.'

Deep in his bunk, Ford Prefect wriggled and turned on to his other side. It wasn't his favourite type of dream because it didn't have Eccentrica Gallumbits, the Triple-Breasted Whore of Eroticon Six, in it, whom many of his dreams did feature. But at least it was a dream. At least he was asleep.

24

Luckily there was a strong updraft in the alley because Arthur hadn't done this sort of thing for a while, at least, not deliberately, and deliberately is exactly the way you are not meant to do it.

He swung down sharply, nearly catching himself a nasty crack on the jaw with the doorstep and tumbled through the air, so suddenly stunned with what a profoundly stupid thing he had just done that he completely forgot the bit about hitting the ground and didn't.

A nice trick, he thought to himself, if you can do it.

The ground was hanging menacingly above his head.

He tried not to think about the ground, what an extraordinarily big thing it was and how much it would hurt him if it decided to stop hanging there and suddenly fell on him. He tried to think nice thoughts about lemurs instead, which was exactly the right thing to do because he couldn't at that moment remember precisely what a lemur was, if it was one of those things that sweep in great majestic herds across the plains of wherever it was or if that was wildebeests, so it was a tricky kind of thing to think nice thoughts about without simply resorting to an icky sort of general well-disposedness towards things, and all this kept his mind well occupied while his body tried to adjust to the fact that it wasn't touching anything.

A Mars bar wrapper fluttered down the alleyway.

After a seeming moment of doubt and indecision it eventually allowed the wind to ease it, fluttering, between him and the ground.

'Arthur . . .'

The ground was still hanging menacingly above his head, and he thought it was probably time to do something about that, such as fall away from it, which is what he did. Slowly. Very very slowly.

As he fell slowly, very very slowly, he closed his eyes – carefully, so as not to jolt anything.

The feel of his eyes closing ran down his whole body. Once it had reached his feet, and the whole of his body was alerted to the fact that his eyes were now closed and was not panicked by it, he slowly, very very slowly, revolved his body one way and his mind the other.

That should sort the ground out.

He could feel the air clear about him now, breezing around him quite cheerfully, untroubled by his being there, and slowly, very very slowly, as from a deep and distant sleep, he opened his eyes.

He had flown before, of course, flown many times on Krikkit until all the birdtalk had driven him scatty, but this was different.

Here he was on his own world, quietly, and without fuss, beyond a slight trembling which could have been attributable to a number of things, being in the air.

Ten or fifteen feet below him was the hard tarmac and a few yards off to the right the yellow street lights of Upper Street.

Luckily the alleyway was dark since the light which

was supposed to see it through the night was on an ingenious timeswitch which meant it came on just before lunchtime and went off again as the evening was beginning to draw in. He was, therefore, safely shrouded in a blanket of dark obscurity.

He slowly, very very slowly, lifted his head to Fenchurch, who was standing in silent breathless amazement, silhouetted in her upstairs doorway.

Her face was inches from his.

'I was about to ask you,' she said in a low trembly voice, 'what you were doing. But then I realized that I could see what you were doing. You were flying. So it seemed,' she went on after a slight wondering pause, 'like a bit of a silly question.'

Arthur said, 'Can you do it?'

'No.'

'Would you like to try?'

She bit her lip and shook her head, not so much to say no, but just in sheer bewilderment. She was shaking like a leaf.

'It's quite easy,' urged Arthur, 'if you don't know how. That's the important bit. Be not at all sure how you're doing it.'

Just to demonstrate how easy it was he floated away down the alley, fell upwards quite dramatically and bobbed back down to her like a banknote on a breath of wind.

'Ask me how I did that.'

'How . . . did you do that?'

'No idea. Not a clue.'

She shrugged in bewilderment. 'So how can I . . .?'

Arthur bobbed down a little lower and held out his hand.

'I want you to try,' he said, 'to step on to my hand. Just one foot.'

'What?'

'Try it.'

Nervously, hesitantly, almost, she told herself, as if she was trying to step on to the hand of someone who was floating in front of her in midair, she stepped on to his hand.

'Now the other.'

'What?'

'Take the weight off your back foot.'

'I can't.'

'Try it.'

'Like this?'

'Like that.'

Nervously, hesitantly, almost, she told herself, as if— She stopped telling herself what what she was doing was like because she had a feeling she didn't altogether want to know.

She fixed her eyes very very firmly on the guttering of the roof of the decrepit warehouse opposite which had been annoying her for weeks because it was clearly going to fall off and she wondered if anyone was going to do anything about it or whether she ought to say something to somebody, and didn't think for a moment about the fact that she was standing on the hands of someone who wasn't standing on anything at all.

'Now,' said Arthur, 'take your weight off your left foot.'

She thought that the warehouse belonged to the carpet company who had their offices round the corner, and took her weight off her left foot, so she should probably go and see them about the gutter.

'Now,' said Arthur, 'take the weight off your right foot.'

'I can't.'

'Try.'

She hadn't seen the guttering from quite this angle before, and it looked to her now as if as well as the mud and gunge up there there might also be a bird's nest. If she leaned forward just a little and took her weight off her right foot, she could probably see it more clearly.

Arthur was alarmed to see that someone down in the alley was trying to steal her bicycle. He particularly didn't want to get involved in an argument at the moment and hoped that the guy would do it quietly and not look up.

He had the quiet shifty look of someone who habitually stole bicycles in alleys and habitually didn't expect to find their owners hovering several feet above them. He was relaxed by both these habits, and went about his job with purpose and concentration, and when he found that the bike was unarguably bound by hoops of tungsten carbide to an iron bar embedded in concrete, he peacefully bent both its wheels and went on his way.

Arthur let out a long-held breath.

'See what a piece of eggshell I have found you,' said Fenchurch in his ear.

25

Those who are regular followers of the doings of Arthur Dent may have received an impression of his character and habits which, while it includes the truth and, of course, nothing but the truth, falls somewhat short, in its composition, of the whole truth in all its glorious aspects.

And the reasons for this are obvious. Editing, selection, the need to balance that which is interesting with that which is relevant and cut out all the tedious happenstance.

Like this, for instance. 'Arthur Dent went to bed. He went up the stairs, all fifteen of them, opened the door, went into his room, took off his shoes and socks and then all the rest of his clothes one by one and left them in a neatly crumpled heap on the floor. He put on his pyjamas, the blue ones with the stripe. He washed his face and hands, cleaned his teeth, went to the lavatory, realized that he had once again got this all in the wrong order, had to wash his hands again and went to bed. He read for fifteen minutes, spending the first ten minutes of that trying to work out where in the book he had got to the previous night, then he turned out the light and within a minute or so more was asleep.

'It was dark. He lay on his left side for a good hour.

'After that he moved restlessly in his sleep for a moment and then turned over to sleep on his right side. Another hour after this his eyes flickered briefly and he slightly scratched his nose, though there was still a good twenty minutes to go before he turned back on to his left side. And so he whiled the night away, sleeping.

'At four he got up and went to the lavatory again. He opened the door to the lavatory . . .' and so on.

It's guff. It doesn't advance the action. It makes for nice fat books such as the American market thrives on, but it doesn't actually get you anywhere. You don't, in short, want to know.

But there are other omissions as well, beside the teethcleaning and trying to find fresh socks variety, and in some of these people have often seemed inordinately interested.

What, they want to know, about all that stuff off in the wings with Arthur and Trillian, did that ever get anywhere?

To which the answer is, of course, mind your own business.

And what, they say, was he up to all those nights on the planet Krikkit? Just because the planet didn't have Fuolornis Fire Dragons or Dire Straits doesn't mean that everyone just sat up every night reading.

Or to take a more specific example, what about the night after the committee meeting party on Prehistoric Earth, when Arthur found himself sitting on a hillside watching the moon rise over the softly burning trees in company with a beautiful young girl called Mella, recently escaped from a lifetime of staring every morning at a hundred nearly identical photographs of moodily lit tubes of toothpaste in the art department of an advertising agency on the planet Golgafrincham? What then? What happened next? And the answer is, of course, that the book ended.

The next one didn't resume the story till five years later, and you can, claim some, take discretion too far. 'This Arthur Dent,' comes the cry from the furthest reaches of the Galaxy, and has even now been found inscribed on a mysterious deep space probe thought to originate from an alien galaxy at a distance too hideous to contemplate, 'what is he, man or mouse? Is he interested in nothing more than tea and the wider issues of life? Has he no spirit? Has he no passion? Does he not, to put it in a nutshell, fuck?'

Those who wish to know should read on. Others may wish to skip on to the last chapter which is a good bit and has Marvin in it.

26

Arthur Dent allowed himself for an unworthy moment to think, as they drifted up, that he very much hoped that his friends who had always found him pleasant but dull, or more latterly, odd but dull, were having a good time in the pub, but that was the last time, for a while, that he thought of them.

They drifted up, spiralling slowly around each other, like sycamore seeds falling from sycamore trees in the autumn, except going the other way.

And as they drifted up their minds sang with the ecstatic knowledge that either what they were doing was completely and utterly and totally impossible or that physics had a lot of catching up to do.

Physics shook its head and, looking the other way, concentrated on keeping the cars going along the Euston Road and out towards the Westway flyover, on keeping the streetlights lit and on making sure that when somebody on Baker Street dropped a cheeseburger it went splat upon the ground.

Dwindling headily beneath them, the beaded strings of lights of London – London, Arthur had to keep reminding himself, not the strangely coloured fields of Krikkit on the remote fringes of the galaxy, lighted freckles of which faintly spanned the opening sky above them, but London – swayed, swaying and turning, turned.

'Try a swoop,' he called to Fenchurch.

'What?'

Her voice seemed strangely clear but distant in all the vast empty air. It was breathy and faint with disbelief – all those things, clear, faint, distant, breathy, all at the same time.

'We're flying . . .' she said.

'A trifle,' called Arthur, 'think nothing of it. Try a swoop.'

'A sw—'

Her hand caught his, and in a second her weight caught it too, and stunningly, she was gone, tumbling beneath him, clawing wildly at nothing.

Physics glanced at Arthur, and clotted with horror he was gone too, sick with giddy dropping, every part of him screaming but his voice.

They plummeted because this was London and you really couldn't do this sort of thing here.

He couldn't catch her because this was London, and not a million miles from here, seven hundred and fifty-six, to be exact, in Pisa, Galileo had clearly demonstrated that two falling bodies fall at exactly the same rate of acceleration irrespective of their relative weights.

They fell.

Arthur realized as he fell, giddily and sickeningly, that if he was going to hang around in the sky believing everything that the Italians had to say about physics when they couldn't even keep a simple tower straight, that they were in dead trouble, and damn well did fall faster than Fenchurch.

He grappled her from above, and fumbled for a tight grip on her shoulders. He got it.

Fine. They were now falling together, which was all very sweet and romantic, but didn't solve the basic problem, which was that they were falling, and the ground wasn't waiting around to see if he had any more clever tricks up his sleeve, but was coming up to meet them like an express train.

He couldn't support her weight, he hadn't anything he could support it with or against. The only thing he could think was that they were obviously going to die, and if he wanted anything other than the obvious to happen he was going to have to do something other than the obvious. Here he felt he was on familiar territory.

He let go of her, pushed her away, and when she turned her face to him in a gasp of stunned horror, caught her little finger with his little finger and swung her back upwards, tumbling clumsily up after her.

'Shit,' she said, as she sat panting and breathless on absolutely nothing at all, and when she had recovered herself they fled on up into the night.

Just below cloud level they paused and scanned where they had impossibly come. The ground was something not to regard with any too firm or steady an eye, but merely to glance at, as it were, in passing.

Fenchurch tried some little swoops, daringly, and found that if she judged herself just right against a body of wind she could pull off some really quite dazzling ones with a little pirouette at the end, followed by a little drop which made her dress billow around her, and this is where readers who are keen to know what Marvin and Ford Prefect have been up to all this while should look ahead to later chapters, because Arthur now could wait no longer and helped her take it off.

It drifted down and away, whipped by the wind until it was a speck which finally vanished, and for various complicated reasons revolutionized the life of a family in Hounslow, over whose washing line it was discovered draped in the morning.

In a mute embrace, they drifted up till they were swimming amongst the misty wraiths of moisture that you can see feathering around the wings of an aeroplane but never feel because you are sitting warm inside the stuffy aeroplane and looking through the little scratchy Perspex window while somebody else's son tries patiently to pour warm milk into your shirt.

Arthur and Fenchurch could feel them, wispy cold and thin, wreathing round their bodies, very cold, very thin. They felt, even Fenchurch, now protected from the elements by only a couple of fragments from Marks and Spencer, that if they were not going to let the force of gravity bother them, then mere cold or paucity of atmosphere could go and whistle.

The two fragments from Marks and Spencer which, as Fenchurch rose now into the misty body of the clouds, Arthur removed very very slowly, which is the only way it's possible to do it when you're flying and also not using your hands, went on to create considerable havoc in the morning in, respectively, counting from top to bottom, Isleworth and Richmond.

They were in the cloud for a long time, because it was stacked very high, and when finally they emerged wetly above it, Fenchurch slowly spinning like a starfish lapped by a rising tidepool, they found that above the clouds is where the night gets seriously moonlit.

The light is darkly brilliant. There are different mountains up there, but they are mountains, with their own white arctic snows.

They had emerged at the top of the high-stacked cumulo-nimbus, and now began lazily to drift down its contours, as Fenchurch eased Arthur in turn from his clothes, prised him free of them till all were gone, winding their surprised way down into the enveloping whiteness.

She kissed him, kissed his neck, his chest, and soon they were drifting on, turning slowly, in a kind of speechless T-shape, which might have caused even a

Fuolornis Fire Dragon, had one flown past, replete with pizza, to flap its wings and cough a little.

There were, however, no Fuolornis Fire Dragons in the clouds nor could there be for, like the dinosaurs, the dodos, and the Greater Drubbered Wintwock of Stegbartle Major in the Constellation Fraz, and unlike the Boeing 747 which is in plentiful supply, they are sadly extinct, and the Universe shall never know their like again.

The reason that a Boeing 747 crops up rather unexpectedly in the above list is not unconnected with the fact that something very similar happened in the lives of Arthur and Fenchurch a moment or two later.

They are big things, terrifyingly big. You know when one is in the air with you. There is a thunderous attack of air, a moving wall of screaming wind, and you get tossed aside, if you are foolish enough to be doing anything remotely like what Arthur and Fenchurch were doing in its close vicinity, like butterflies in the Blitz.

This time, however, there was a heart-sickening fall or loss of nerve, a re-grouping moments later and a wonderful new idea enthusiastically signalled through the buffeting noise.

Mrs E. Kapelsen of Boston, Massachusetts was an elderly lady, indeed, she felt her life was nearly at an end. She had seen a lot of it, been puzzled by some, but, she was a little uneasy to feel at this late stage, bored by too much. It had all been very pleasant, but perhaps a little too explicable, a little too routine.

With a sigh she flipped up the little plastic window shutter and looked out over the wing.

At first she thought she ought to call the stewardess, but then she thought no, damn it, definitely not, this was for her, and her alone.

By the time her two inexplicable people finally slipped back off the wing and tumbled into the slip-stream she had cheered up an awful lot.

She was mostly immensely relieved to think that virtually everything that anybody had ever told her was wrong.

* * *

The following morning Arthur and Fenchurch slept very late in the alley despite the continual wail of furniture being restored.

The following night they did it all over again, only this time with Sony Walkmen.

27

'This is all very wonderful,' said Fenchurch a few days later. 'But I do need to know what has happened to me. You see, there's this difference between us. That you lost something and found it again, and I found something and lost it. I need to find it again.'

She had to go out for the day, so Arthur settled down for a day of telephoning.

Murray Bost Henson was a journalist on one of the papers with small pages and big print. It would be pleasant to be able to say that he was none the worse for this, but sadly, this was not the case. He happened to be the only journalist that Arthur knew, so Arthur phoned him anyway.

'Arthur, my old soup spoon, my old silver tureen, how particularly stunning to hear from you. Someone told me you'd gone off into space or something.'

Murray had his own special kind of conversation language which he had invented for his own use, and which no one else was able to speak or even to follow. Hardly any of it meant anything at all. The bits which did mean anything were often so wonderfully buried that no one could ever spot them slipping past in the avalanche of nonsense. The time when you did find out, later, which bits he did mean, was often a bad time for all concerned.

'What?' said Arthur.

'Just a rumour, my old elephant tusk, my little green baize card table, just a rumour. Probably means nothing at all, but I may need a quote from you.'

'Nothing to say, just pub talk.'

'We thrive on it, my old prosthetic limb, we thrive on it. Plus it would fit like a whatsit in one of those other things with the other stories of the week, so it could be just to have you denying it. Excuse me, something has just fallen out of my ear.'

There was a slight pause, at the end of which Murray Bost Henson came back on the line sounding genuinely shaken.

'Just remembered,' he said, 'what an odd evening I had last night. Anyway my old, I won't say what, how do you feel about having ridden on Halley's Comet?'

'I haven't,' said Arthur with a suppressed sigh, 'ridden on Halley's Comet.'

'OK. How do you feel about not having ridden on Halley's Comet?'

'Pretty relaxed, Murray.'

There was a pause while Murray wrote this down.

'Good enough for me, Arthur, good enough for Ethel and me and the chickens. Fits in with the general weirdness of the week. Week of the Weirdos, we're thinking of calling it. Good, eh?'

'Very good.'

'Got a ring to it. First we have this man it always rains on.'

'What?'

'It's the absolute stocking-top truth. All documented in his little black book, it all checks out at every single fun-loving level. The Met Office is going ice-cold thick banana whips, and funny little men in white coats are flying in from all over the world with their little rulers and boxes and drip feeds. This man is the bee's knees, Arthur, he is the wasp's nipples. He is, I would go so far as to say, the entire set of erogenous zones of every major flying insect of the Western world. We're calling him the Rain God. Nice, eh?'

'I think I've met him.'

'Good ring to it. What did you say?'

'I may have met him. Complains all the time, yes?'

'Incredible! You met the Rain God?'

'If it's the same guy. I told him to stop complaining and show someone his book.'

There was an impressed pause from Murray Bost Henson's end of the phone.

'Well, you did a bundle. An absolute bundle has absolutely been done by you. Listen, do you know how much a tour operator is paying that guy not to go to Malaga this year? I mean forget irrigating the Sahara and boring stuff like that, this guy has a whole new *career* ahead of him, just avoiding places for money. The man's turning into a monster, Arthur, we might even have to make him win the bingo.

'Listen, we may want to do a feature on you, Arthur, the Man Who Made the Rain God Rain. Got a ring to it, eh?'

'A nice one, but . . .'

'We may need to photograph you under a garden shower, but that'll be OK. Where are you?'

'Er, I'm in Islington. Listen, Murray . . .'

'Islington!'

'Yes . . .'

'Well, what about the *real* weirdness of the week, the real seriously loopy stuff. You know anything about these flying people?'

'No.'

'You must have. This is the real seethingly crazy one. This is the real meatballs in the batter. Locals are phoning in all the time to say there's this couple who go flying nights. We've got guys down in our photo labs working through the night to put together a genuine photograph. You must have heard.'

'No.'

'Arthur, where have you been? Oh, space, right, I got your quote. But that was months ago. Listen, it's night after night this week, my old cheesegrater, right on your patch. This couple just fly around the sky and start doing all kinds of stuff. And I don't mean looking through walls or pretending to be box-girder bridges. You don't know anything?'

'No.'

'Arthur, it's been almost inexpressibly delicious conversing with you, chumbum, but I have to go. I'll send the guy with the camera and the hose. Give me the address, I'm ready and writing.'

'Listen, Murray, I called to ask you something.'

'I have a lot to do.'

'I just wanted to find out something about the dolphins.'

'No story. Last year's news. Forget 'em. They're gone.'

'It's important.'

'Listen, no one will touch it. You can't sustain a story, you know, when the only news is the continuing absence of whatever it is the story's about. Not our territory anyway, try the Sundays. Maybe they'll run a little "Whatever Happened to 'Whatever Happened to the Dolphins'" story in a couple of years, around August. But what's anybody going to do now? "Dolphins Still Gone"? "Continuing Dolphin Absence"? "Dolphins – Further Days Without Them"? The story dies, Arthur. It lies down and kicks its little feet in the air and presently goes to the great golden spike in the sky, my old fruitbat.'

'Murray, I'm not interested in whether it's a story. I just want to find out how I can get in touch with that guy in California who claims to know something about it. I thought you might know.'

28

'People are beginning to talk,' said Fenchurch that evening, after they had hauled her cello in.

'Not only talk,' said Arthur, 'but print, in big bold letters under the bingo prizes. Which is why I thought I'd better get these.'

He showed her the long narrow booklets of airline tickets.

'Arthur!' she said, hugging him. 'Does that mean you managed to talk to him?'

'I have had a day,' said Arthur, 'of extreme telephonic exhaustion. I have spoken to virtually every department of virtually every paper in Fleet Street, and I finally tracked his number down.'

'You've obviously been working hard, you're drenched with sweat, poor darling.'

'Not with sweat,' said Arthur wearily. 'A photographer's just been. I tried to argue, but – never mind, the point is, yes.'

'You spoke to him.'

'I spoke to his wife. She said he was too weird to come to the phone right now and could I call back.'

He sat down heavily, realized he was missing something and went to the fridge to find it.

'Want a drink?'

'Would commit murder to get one. I always know I'm in for a tough time when my 'cello teacher looks me up and down and says, "Ah yes, my dear, I think a little Tchaikovsky today."'

'I called again,' said Arthur, 'and she said that he was 3.2 light-years from the phone and I should call back.'

'Ah.'

'I called again. She said the situation had improved. He was now a mere 2.6 light-years from the phone but it was still a long way to shout.'

'You don't suppose,' said Fenchurch, doubtfully, 'that there's anyone else we can talk to?'

'It gets worse,' said Arthur. 'I spoke to someone on a science magazine who actually knows him, and he said that John Watson will not only believe, but will actually have absolute proof, often dictated to him by angels with golden beards and green wings and Dr Scholl footwear, that the month's most fashionable silly theory is true. For people who question the validity of these visions he will triumphantly produce the clogs in question, and that's as far as you get.'

'I didn't realize it was that bad,' said Fenchurch quietly. She fiddled listlessly with the tickets.

'I phoned Mrs Watson again,' said Arthur. 'Her name,

by the way, and you may wish to know this, is Arcane Jill.'

'I see.'

'I'm glad you see. I thought you mightn't believe any of this, so when I called her this time I used the telephone answering machine to record the call.'

He went across to the telephone machine and fiddled and fumed with all its buttons for a while, because it was the one which was particularly recommended by *Which?* magazine and is almost impossible to use without going mad.

'Here it is,' he said at last, wiping the sweat from his brow.

The voice was thin and crackly with its journey to a geostationary satellite and back, but was also hauntingly calm.

'Perhaps I should explain,' Arcane Jill Watson's voice said, 'that the phone is in fact in a room that he never comes into. It's in the Asylum, you see. Wonko the Sane does not like to enter the Asylum and so he does not. I feel you should know this because it may save you phoning. If you would like to meet him, this is very easily arranged. All you have to do is walk in. He will only meet people outside the Asylum.'

Arthur's voice, at its most mystified: 'I'm sorry, I don't understand. Where is the asylum?'

'*Where* is the Asylum?' Arcane Jill Watson again. 'Have you ever read the instructions on a packet of toothpicks?'

On the tape, Arthur's voice had to admit that he had not.

'You may want to do that. You may find that it clarifies things for you a little. You may find that it indicates to you where the Asylum is. Thank you.'

The sound of the phone line went dead. Arthur turned the machine off.

'Well, I suppose we can regard that as an invitation,' he said with a shrug. 'I actually managed to get the address from the guy on the science magazine.'

Fenchurch looked up at him again with a thoughtful frown, and looked at the tickets again.

'Do you think it's worth it?' she said.

'Well,' said Arthur, 'the one thing that everyone I spoke to agreed on, apart from the fact that they all thought he was barking mad, is that he does know more than any man living about dolphins.'

29

'This is an important announcement. This is flight 121 to Los Angeles. If your travel plans today do not include Los Angeles, now would be the perfect time to disembark.'

30

They rented a car in Los Angeles from one of the places that rents out cars that other people have thrown away.

'Getting it to go round corners is a bit of a problem,' said the guy behind the sunglasses as he handed them the keys, 'sometimes it's simpler just to get out and find a car that's going in that direction.'

They stayed for one night in a hotel on Sunset Boulevard which someone had told them they would enjoy being puzzled by.

'Everyone there is either English or odd or both. They've got a swimming pool where you can go and watch English rock stars reading *Language, Truth and Logic* for the photographers.'

It was true. There was one and that was exactly what he was doing.

The garage attendant didn't think much of their car, but that was fine because they didn't either.

Late in the evening they drove through the Hollywood hills along Mulholland Drive and stopped to look out first over the dazzling sea of floating light that is Los Angeles, and later stopped to look across the dazzling sea of floating light that is the San Fernando Valley. They agreed that the sense of dazzle stopped immediately at the back of their eyes and didn't touch any other part of them and came away strangely unsatisfied by the spectacle. As dramatic seas of light went, it was fine, but light is meant to illuminate something, and having driven through what this particularly dramatic sea of light was illuminating they didn't think much of it.

They slept late and restlessly and awoke at lunchtime when it was stupidly hot.

They drove out along the freeway to Santa Monica for their first look at the Pacific Ocean, the ocean which Wonko the Sane spent all his days and a good deal of his nights looking at.

'Someone told me,' said Fenchurch, 'that they once overheard two old ladies on this beach, doing what we're doing, looking at the Pacific Ocean for the first time in their lives. And apparently, after a long pause, one of them said to the other, "You know, it's not as big as I expected."'

Their mood gradually lifted as they walked along the beach in Malibu and watched all the millionaires in their chic shanty huts carefully keeping an eye on each other to check how rich they were each getting.

Their mood lifted further as the sun began to move down the western half of the sky, and by the time they were back in their rattling car and driving towards a sunset that no one of any sensibility would dream of building a city like Los Angeles in front of, they were suddenly feeling astonishingly and irrationally happy and didn't even mind that the terrible old car radio would only play two stations, and those simultaneously. So what, they were both playing good rock and roll.

'I know that he will be able to help us,' said Fenchurch determinedly. 'I know he will. What's his name again, that he likes to be called?'

'Wonko the Sane.'

'I know that he will be able to help us.'

Arthur wondered if he would and hoped that he would, and hoped that what Fenchurch had lost could be found here, on this Earth, whatever this Earth might prove to be.

He hoped, as he had hoped continually and fervently since the time they had talked together on the banks of the Serpentine, that he would not be called upon to try and remember something that he had very firmly and deliberately buried in the furthest recesses of his memory, where he hoped it would cease to nag at him.

* * *

In Santa Barbara they stopped at a fish restaurant in what seemed to be a converted warehouse.

Fenchurch had red mullet and said it was delicious.

Arthur had a swordfish steak and said it made him angry.

He grabbed a passing waitress by the arm and berated her.

'Why's this fish so bloody good?' he demanded, angrily.

'Please excuse my friend,' said Fenchurch to the startled waitress. 'I think he's having a nice day at last.'

31

If you took a couple of David Bowies and stuck one of the David Bowies on the top of the other David Bowie, then attached another David Bowie to the end of each of the arms of the upper of the first two David Bowies and wrapped the whole business up in a dirty beach robe you would then have something which didn't exactly look like John Watson, but which those who knew him would find hauntingly familiar.

He was tall and he gangled.

When he sat in his deckchair gazing at the Pacific, not so much with any kind of wild surmise any longer as with a peaceful deep dejection, it was a little difficult to tell exactly where the deckchair ended and he began, and you would hesitate to put your hand on, say, his forearm in case the whole structure suddenly collapsed with a snap and took your thumb off.

But his smile when he turned it on you was quite remarkable. It seemed to be composed of all the worst things that life can do to you, but which, when he briefly reassembled them in that particular order on his face, made you suddenly feel, 'Oh. Well, that's all right, then.'

When he spoke, you were glad that he used the smile that made you feel like that pretty often.

'Oh yes,' he said, 'they come and see me. They sit right here. They sit right where you're sitting.' He was talking of the angels with the golden beards and green wings and Dr Scholl sandals.

'They eat nachos which they say they can't get where they come from. They do a lot of coke and are very wonderful about a whole range of things.'

'Do they?' said Arthur. 'Are they? So, er . . . when is this, then? When do they come?'

He gazed out at the Pacific as well. There were little sandpipers running along the margin of the shore which seemed to have this problem: they needed to find their food in the sand which a wave had just washed over, but they couldn't bear to get their feet wet. To deal with this problem they ran with an odd kind of movement as if they'd been constructed by somebody very clever in Switzerland.

Fenchurch was sitting on the sand, idly drawing patterns in it with her fingers.

'Weekends, mostly,' said Wonko the Sane, 'on little scooters. They are great machines.' He smiled.

'I see,' said Arthur. 'I see.'

A tiny cough from Fenchurch attracted his attention and he looked round at her. She had scratched a little stick figure drawing in the sand of the two of them in the clouds. For a moment he thought she was trying to get him excited, then he realized that she was rebuking him. 'Who are we,' she was saying, 'to say he's mad?'

His house was certainly peculiar, and since this was the first thing that Fenchurch and Arthur had encountered it would help to know what it was like.

What it was like was this:

It was inside out.

Actually inside out, to the extent that they had to park on the carpet.

All along what one would normally call the outer wall, which was decorated in a tasteful interior-designed pink, were bookshelves, also a couple of those odd three-legged tables with semi-circular tops which stand in such a way as to suggest that someone just dropped the wall straight through them, and pictures which were clearly designed to soothe.

Where it got really odd was the roof.

It folded back on itself like something that Maurits C. Escher, had he been given to hard nights on the town, which it is no part of this narrative's purpose to suggest was the case, though it is sometimes hard, looking at his pictures, particularly the one with all the awkward steps, not to wonder, might have dreamed up after having been on one, for the little chandeliers which should have been hanging inside were on the outside pointing up.

Confusing.

The sign above the front door said, 'Come Outside', and so, nervously, they had.

Inside, of course, was where the Outside was. Rough brickwork, nicely done pointing, guttering in good repair, a garden path, a couple of small trees, some rooms leading off.

And the inner walls stretched down, folded curiously, and opened at the end as if, by an optical illusion which would have had Maurits C. Escher frowning and wondering how it was done, to enclose the Pacific Ocean itself.

'Hello,' said John Watson, Wonko the Sane.

Good, they thought to themselves, 'Hello' is something we can cope with.

'Hello,' they said, and all surprisingly was smiles.

For quite a while he seemed curiously reluctant to talk about the dolphins, looking oddly distracted and saying, 'I forget . . .' whenever they were mentioned, and had shown them quite proudly round the eccentricities of his house.

'It gives me pleasure,' he said, 'in a curious kind of way, and does nobody any harm,' he continued, 'that a competent optician couldn't correct.'

They liked him. He had an open, engaging quality and seemed able to mock himself before anybody else did.

'Your wife,' said Arthur, looking around, 'mentioned some toothpicks.' He said it with a hunted look, as if he was worried that she might suddenly leap out from behind the door and mention them again.

Wonko the Sane laughed. It was a light easy laugh, and sounded like one he had used a lot before and was happy with.

'Ah yes,' he said, 'that's to do with the day I finally realized that the world had gone totally mad and built the Asylum to put it in, poor thing, and hoped it would get better.'

This was the point at which Arthur began to feel a little nervous again.

'Here,' said Wonko the Sane, 'we are outside the Asylum.' He pointed again at the rough brickwork, the pointing and the guttering. 'Go through that door,' he pointed at the first door through which they had originally entered, 'and you go into the Asylum. I've tried to decorate it nicely to keep the inmates happy, but there's very little one can do. I never go in there now myself. If ever I am tempted, which these days I rarely am, I simply look at the sign written over the door and I shy away.'

'That one?' said Fenchurch, pointing, rather puzzled, at a blue plaque with some instructions written on it.

'Yes. They are the words that finally turned me into the hermit I have now become. It was quite sudden. I saw them, and I knew what I had to do.'

The sign said:

Hold stick near centre of its length. Moisten pointed end in mouth. Insert in tooth space, blunt end next to gum. Use gentle in–out motion.

'It seemed to me,' said Wonko the Sane, 'that any civilization that had so far lost its head as to need to include a set of detailed instructions for use in a packet of toothpicks was no longer a civilization in which I could live and stay sane.'

He gazed out at the Pacific again, as if daring it to rave and gibber at him, but it lay there calmly and played with the sandpipers.

'And in case it crossed your mind to wonder, as I can see how it possibly might, I am completely sane. Which is why I call myself Wonko the Sane, just to reassure people on this point. Wonko is what my mother called me when I was a kid and clumsy and knocked things over, and sane is what I am, and how,' he added, with one of his smiles that made you feel, 'Oh. Well, that's all right, then.', 'I intend to remain. Shall we go onto the beach and see what we have to talk about?'

They went out onto the beach, which was where he started talking about angels with golden beards and green wings and Dr Scholl sandals.

'About the dolphins . . .' said Fenchurch gently, hopefully.

'I can show you the sandals,' said Wonko the Sane.

'I wonder, do you know . . .'

'Would you like me to show you,' said Wonko the

Sane, 'the sandals? I have them. I'll get them. They are made by the Dr Scholl company, and the angels say that they particularly suit the terrain they have to work in. They say they run a concession stand by the message. When I say I don't know what that means they say, "No, you don't," and laugh. Well, I'll get them anyway.'

As he walked back towards the inside, or the outside depending on how you looked at it, Arthur and Fenchurch looked at each other in a wondering and slightly desperate sort of way, then each shrugged and idly drew figures in the sand.

'How are the feet today?' said Arthur quietly.

'OK. It doesn't feel so odd in the sand. Or in the water. The water touches them perfectly. I just think this isn't our world.'

She shrugged.

'What do you think he meant,' she said, 'by the message?'

'I don't know,' said Arthur, though the memory of a man called Prak who laughed at him continuously kept nagging at him.

When Wonko returned he was carrying something that stunned Arthur. Not the sandals, they were perfectly ordinary wooden-bottomed sandals.

'I just thought you'd like to see,' he said, 'what angels wear on their feet. Just out of curiosity. I'm not trying to prove anything, by the way. I'm a scientist and I know what constitutes proof. But the reason I call myself by my childhood name is to remind myself that a scientist must also be absolutely like a child. If he sees a thing, he must say that he sees it, whether it was what he thought he was going to see or not. See first, think later, then test. But always see first. Otherwise you will only see what you were expecting. Most scientists forget that. I'll show you something to demonstrate that later.

So, the other reason I call myself Wonko the Sane is so that people will think I am a fool. That allows me to say what I see when I see it. You can't possibly be a scientist if you mind people thinking that you're a fool. Anyway, I also thought you might like to see this.'

This was the thing that Arthur had been stunned to see him carrying, for it was a wonderful silver-grey glass fish bowl, seemingly identical to the one in Arthur's bedroom.

Arthur had been trying for some thirty seconds now, without success, to say, 'Where did you get that?' sharply, and with a gasp in his voice.

Finally his time had come, but he missed it by a millisecond.

'Where did you get that?' said Fenchurch, sharply and with a gasp in her voice.

Arthur glanced at Fenchurch sharply and with a gasp in his voice said, 'What? Have you seen one of these before?'

'Yes,' she said, 'I've got one. Or at least did have. Russell nicked it to put his golfballs in. I don't know where it came from, just that I was angry with Russell for nicking it. Why, have you got one?'

'Yes, it was . . .'

They both became aware that Wonko the Sane was glancing sharply backwards and forwards between them, and trying to get a gasp in edgeways.

'*You* have one of these too?' he said to both of them.

'Yes.' They both said it.

He looked long and calmly at each of them, then he held up the bowl to catch the light of the Californian sun.

The bowl seemed almost to sing with the sun, to chime with the intensity of its light, and cast darkly brilliant rainbows around the sand and upon them. He turned it, and turned it. They could see quite clearly in the fine tracery of its etchwork the words 'So Long, and Thanks For All The Fish.'

'Do you know,' asked Wonko quietly, 'what it is?'

They each shook their heads slowly, and with wonder, almost hypnotized by the flashing of the lightning shadows in the grey glass.

'It is a farewell gift from the dolphins,' said Wonko in a low quiet voice, 'the dolphins whom I loved and studied, and swam with, and fed with fish, and even tried to learn their language, a task which they seemed to make impossibly difficult, considering the fact that I now realize they were perfectly capable of communicating in ours if they decided they wanted to.'

He shook his head with a slow, slow smile, and then looked again at Fenchurch, and then at Arthur.

'Have you . . .' he said to Arthur, 'what have you done with yours? May I ask you that?'

'Er, I keep a fish in it,' said Arthur, slightly embarrassed. 'I happened to have this fish I was wondering what to do with, and er, there was this bowl.' He tailed off.

'You've done nothing else? No,' he said, 'if you had, you would know.' He shook his head again.

'My wife kept wheatgerm in ours,' resumed Wonko, with some new tone in his voice, 'until last night . . .'

'What,' said Arthur slowly and hushedly, 'happened last night?'

'We ran out of wheatgerm,' said Wonko, evenly. 'My wife,' he added, 'has gone to get some more.' He seemed lost with his own thoughts for a moment.

'And what happened then?' said Fenchurch, in the same breathless tone.

'I washed it,' said Wonko. 'I washed it very carefully, very very carefully, removing every last speck of wheatgerm, then I dried it slowly with a lint-free cloth, slowly, carefully, turning it over and over. Then I held it to my ear. Have you . . . have you held one to your ear?'

They both shook their heads, again slowly, again dumbly.

'Perhaps,' he said, 'you should.'

32

The deep roar of the ocean.

The break of waves on further shores than thought can find.

The silent thunders of the deep.

And from among it, voices calling, and yet not voices, humming trillings, wordlings, the half-articulated songs of thought.

Greetings, waves of greetings, sliding back down into the inarticulate, words breaking together.

A crash of sorrow on the shores of Earth.

Waves of joy on – where? A world indescribably found, indescribably arrived at, indescribably wet, a song of water.

A fugue of voices now, clamouring for explanations, of a disaster unavertable, a world to be destroyed, a surge of helplessness, a spasm of despair, a dying fall, again the break of words.

And then the fling of hope, the finding of a shadow Earth in the implications of enfolded time, submerged dimensions, the pull of parallels, the deep pull, the spin of will, the hurl and split of it, the flight. A new Earth pulled into replacement, the dolphins gone.

Then stunningly a single voice, quite clear.

'This bowl was brought to you by the Campaign to Save the Humans. We bid you farewell.'

And then the sound of long, heavy, perfectly grey bodies rolling away into an unknown fathomless deep, quietly giggling.

33

That night they stayed Outside the Asylum and watched TV from inside it.

'This is what I wanted you to see,' said Wonko the Sane when the news came around again, 'an old colleague of mine. He's over in your country running an investigation. Just watch.'

It was a press conference.

'I'm afraid I can't comment on the name Rain God at this present time, and we are calling him an example of a Spontaneous Para-Causal Meteorological Phenomenon.'

'Can you tell us what that means?'

'I'm not altogether sure. Let's be straight here. If we find something we can't understand, we like to call it something you can't understand, or indeed pronounce. I mean if we just let you go around calling him a Rain God, then that suggests that you know something we don't, and I'm afraid we couldn't have that.

'No, first we have to call it something which says it's ours, not yours, then we set about finding some way of proving it's not what you said it is, but something we say it is.

'And if it turns out that you're right, you'll still be wrong, because we will simply call him a . . . er, "Supernormal . . ." – not paranormal or supernatural because you think you know what those mean now, no, a "Supernormal Incremental Precipitation Inducer". We'll probably want to shove a "Quasi" in there somewhere to protect ourselves. Rain God! Huh, never heard such nonsense in my life. Admittedly, you wouldn't catch me going on holiday with him. Thanks, that'll be all for now, other than to say "Hi!" to Wonko if he's watching.'

34

On the way home there was a woman sitting next to them on the plane who was looking at them rather oddly.

They talked quietly to themselves.

'I still have to know,' said Fenchurch, 'and I strongly feel that you know something that you're not telling me.'

Arthur sighed and took out a piece of paper.

'Do you have a pencil?' he said. She dug around and found one.

'What are you doing, sweetheart?' she said, after he had spent twenty minutes frowning, chewing the pencil, scribbling on the paper, crossing things out, scribbling again, chewing the pencil again and grunting irritably to himself.

'Trying to remember an address someone once gave me.'

'Your life would be an awful lot simpler,' she said, 'if you bought yourself an address book.'

Finally he passed the paper to her.

'You look after it,' he said.

She looked at it. Among all the scratchings and crossings out were the words 'Quentulus Quazgar Mountains. Sevorbeupstry. Planet of Preliumtarn. Sun Zarss. Galactic Sector QQ7 Active J Gamma.'

'And what's there?'

'Apparently,' said Arthur, 'it's God's Final Message to His Creation.'

'That sounds a bit more like it,' said Fenchurch. 'How do we get there?'

'You really . . .?'

'Yes,' said Fenchurch firmly, 'I really want to know.'

Arthur looked out of the scratchy little Perspex window at the open sky outside.

'Excuse me,' said the woman who had been looking at them rather oddly, suddenly, 'I hope you don't think I'm rude. I get so bored on these long flights, it's nice to talk to somebody. My name's Enid Kapelsen, I'm from Boston. Tell me, do you fly a lot?'

35

They went to Arthur's house in the West Country, shoved a couple of towels and stuff in a bag, and then sat down to do what every Galactic hitchhiker ends up spending most of his time doing.

They waited for a flying saucer to come by.

'Friend of mine did this for fifteen years,' said Arthur one night as they sat forlornly watching the sky.

'Who was that?'

'Called Ford Prefect.'

He caught himself doing something he had never really expected to do again.

He wondered where Ford Prefect was.

By an extraordinary coincidence, the following day there were two reports in the paper, one concerning the most astonishing incident with a flying saucer, and the other about a series of unseemly riots in pubs.

Ford Prefect turned up the day after that looking hung over and complaining that Arthur never answered the phone.

In fact he looked extremely ill, not merely as if he'd been pulled through a hedge backwards, but as if the hedge was being simultaneously pulled backwards through a combine harvester. He staggered into Arthur's sitting room, waving aside all offers of support, which was an error, because the effort of waving caused him to lose his balance altogether and Arthur had eventually to drag him to the sofa.

'Thank you,' said Ford, 'thank you very much. Have you . . .' he said, and fell asleep for three hours.

'. . . the faintest idea,' he continued suddenly, when he revived, 'how hard it is to tap into the British phone system from the Pleiades? I can see that you haven't, so I'll tell you,' he said, 'over the very large mug of black coffee that you are about to make me.'

He followed Arthur wobbily into the kitchen.

'Stupid operators keep asking you where you're calling from and you try and tell them Letchworth and they say you couldn't be if you're coming in on that circuit. What are you doing?'

'Making you some black coffee.'

'Oh.' Ford seemed oddly disappointed. He looked about the place forlornly.

'What's this?' he said.

'Rice Krispies.'

'And this?'

'Paprika.'

'I see,' said Ford, solemnly, and put the two items back down, one on top of the other, but that didn't seem to balance properly, so he put the other on top of the one and that seemed to work.

'A little space-lagged,' he said. 'What was I saying?'

'About not phoning from Letchworth.'

'I wasn't. I explained this to the lady. "Bugger Letchworth," I said, "if that's your attitude. I am in fact calling from a sales scoutship of the Sirius Cybernetics Corporation, currently on the sub-light-speed leg of a journey between the stars known to your world, though not necessarily to you, dear lady" – I said "dear lady",' explained Ford Prefect, 'because I didn't want her to be offended by my implication that she was an ignorant cretin . . .'

'Tactful,' said Arthur Dent.

'Exactly,' said Ford, 'tactful.'

He frowned.

'Space-lag,' he said, 'is very bad for sub clauses. You'll have to assist me again,' he continued, 'by reminding me what I was talking about.'

'"Between the stars,"' said Arthur, '"known to your world, though not necessarily to you, dear lady, as . . ."'

'"Pleiades Epsilon and Pleiades Zeta,"' concluded Ford triumphantly. 'This conversation lark is quite a gas, isn't it?'

'Have some coffee.'

'Thank you, no. "And the reason," I said, "why I am bothering you with it rather than just dialling direct as I could, because we have some pretty sophisticated telecommunications equipment out here in the Pleiades, I can tell you, is that the penny-pinching son of a starbeast piloting this son of a starbeast starship insists that I call collect. Can you believe that?"'

'And could she?'

'I don't know. She had hung up,' said Ford, 'by this time. So! What do you suppose,' he asked fiercely, 'I did next?'

'I've no idea, Ford,' said Arthur.

'Pity,' said Ford, 'I was hoping you could remind me. I really hate those guys, you know. They really are the creeps of the cosmos, buzzing around the celestial infinite with their junky little machines that never work properly or, when they do, perform functions that no sane man would require of them and,' he added savagely, 'go beep to tell you when they've done it!'

This was perfectly true, and a very respectable view widely held by right-thinking people, who are largely recognizable as being right-thinking people by the mere fact that they hold this view.

The Hitchhiker's Guide to the Galaxy, in a moment of reasoned lucidity which is almost unique among its current tally of five million, nine hundred and seventy-five thousand, five hundred and nine pages, says of the Sirius Cybernetics Corporation products that 'it is very easy to be blinded to the essential uselessness of them by the sense of achievement you get from getting them to work at all.

'In other words – and this is the rock-solid principle on which the whole of the Corporation's Galaxy-wide success is founded – their fundamental design flaws are completely hidden by their superficial design flaws.'

'And this guy,' ranted Ford, 'was on a drive to sell more of them! His five-year mission to seek out and explore strange new worlds, and sell Advanced Music Substitute Systems to their restaurants, elevators and wine bars! Or if they didn't have restaurants, elevators and wine bars yet, to artificially accelerate their civilization growth until they bloody well did have! Where's that coffee!'

'I threw it away.'

'Make some more. I have now remembered what I did next. I saved civilization as we know it. I knew it was something like that.'

He stumbled determinedly back into the sitting room, where he seemed to carry on talking to himself, tripping over the furniture and making beep beep noises.

A couple of minutes later, wearing his very placid face, Arthur followed him.

Ford looked stunned.

'Where have you been?' he demanded.

'Making some coffee,' said Arthur, still wearing his very placid face. He had long ago realized that the only way of being in Ford's company successfully was to keep a large stock of very placid faces and wear them at all times.

'You missed the best bit!' raged Ford. 'You missed the bit where I jumped the guy! Now,' he said, 'I shall have to jump him, all over him!'

He hurled himself recklessly at a chair and broke it.

'It was better,' he said sullenly, 'last time,' and waved vaguely in the direction of another broken chair which he had already got trussed up on the dining table.

'I see,' said Arthur, casting a placid eye over the trussed-up wreckage, 'and, er, what are all the ice cubes for?'

'What?' screamed Ford. 'What? You missed that bit too? That's the suspended animation facility! I put the guy in the suspended animation facility. 'Well, I had to, didn't I?'

'So it would seem,' said Arthur, in his placid voice.

'Don't touch that!!!' yelled Ford.

Arthur, who was about to replace the phone, which was for some mysterious reason lying on the table, off the hook, paused, placidly.

'OK,' said Ford, calming down, 'listen to it.'

Arthur put the phone to his ear.

'It's the speaking clock,' he said.

'Beep, beep, beep,' said Ford, 'is exactly what is being heard all over that guy's ship, while he sleeps, in the ice, going slowly round a little-known moon of Sesefras Magna. The London Speaking Clock!'

'I see,' said Arthur again, and decided that now was the time to ask the big one.

'Why?' he said, placidly.

'With a bit of luck,' said Ford, 'the phone bill will bankrupt the buggers.'

He threw himself, sweating, on to the sofa.

'Anyway,' he said, 'dramatic arrival, don't you think?'

36

The flying saucer in which Ford Prefect had stowed away had stunned the world.

Finally there was no doubt, no possibility of mistake, no hallucinations, no mysterious CIA agents found floating in reservoirs.

This time it was real, it was definite. It was quite definitely definite.

It had come down with a wonderful disregard for anything beneath it and crushed a large area of some of the most expensive real estate in the world, including much of Harrods.

The thing was massive, nearly a mile across, some said, dull silver in colour, pitted, scorched and disfigured with the scars of unnumbered vicious space battles fought with savage forces by the light of suns unknown to man.

A hatchway opened, crashed down through the Harrods Food Halls, demolished Harvey Nichols, and with a final grinding scream of tortured architecture toppled the Sheraton Park Tower.

After a long, heart-stopping moment of internal crashes and grumbles of rending machinery, there marched from it, down the ramp, an immense silver robot, a hundred feet tall.

It held up a hand.

'I come in peace,' it said, adding after a long moment of further grinding, 'take me to your Lizard.'

Ford Prefect, of course, had an explanation for this, as he sat with Arthur and watched the nonstop frenetic news reports on the television, none of which had anything to say other than to record that the thing had done this amount of damage which was valued at that amount of billions of pounds and had killed this totally other number of people, and then say it again, because the robot was doing nothing more than standing there, swaying very slightly, and emitting short incomprehensible error messages.

'It comes from a very ancient democracy, you see . . .'

'You mean, it comes from a world of lizards?'

'No,' said Ford, who by this time was a little more rational and coherent than he had been, having finally had the coffee forced down him, 'nothing so simple. Nothing anything like so straightforward. On its world, the people are people. The leaders are lizards. The people hate the lizards and the lizards rule the people.'

'Odd,' said Arthur, 'I thought you said it was a democracy.'

'I did,' said Ford. 'It is.'

'So,' said Arthur, hoping he wasn't sounding ridiculously obtuse, 'why don't people get rid of the lizards?'

'It honestly doesn't occur to them,' said Ford. 'They've all got the vote, so they all pretty much assume that the government they've voted in more or less approximates to the government they want.'

'You mean they actually *vote* for the lizards?'

'Oh yes,' said Ford with a shrug, 'of course.'

'But,' said Arthur, going for the big one again, 'why?'

'Because if they didn't vote for a lizard,' said Ford, 'the wrong lizard might get in. Got any gin?'

'What?'

'I said,' said Ford, with an increasing air of urgency creeping into his voice, 'have you got any gin?'

'I'll look. Tell me about the lizards.'

Ford shrugged again.

'Some people say that the lizards are the best thing that ever happened to them,' he said. 'They're completely wrong of course, completely and utterly wrong, but someone's got to say it.'

'But that's terrible,' said Arthur.

'Listen, bud,' said Ford, 'if I had one Altairian dollar for every time I heard one bit of the Universe look at another bit of the Universe and say "That's terrible" I wouldn't be sitting here like a lemon looking for a gin. But I haven't and I am. Anyway, what are you looking so placid and moon-eyed for? Are you in love?'

Arthur said yes, he was, and said it placidly.

'With someone who knows where the gin bottle is? Do I get to meet her?'

He did because Fenchurch came in at that moment with a pile of newspapers she'd been into the village to buy. She stopped in astonishment at the wreckage on the table and the wreckage from Betelgeuse on the sofa.

'Where's the gin?' said Ford to Fenchurch. And to Arthur, 'What happened to Trillian, by the way?'

'Er, this is Fenchurch,' said Arthur, awkwardly. 'There was nothing with Trillian, you must have seen her last.'

'Oh, yeah,' said Ford, 'she went off with Zaphod somewhere. They had some kids or something. At least,' he added, 'I think that's what they were. Zaphod's calmed down a lot, you know.'

'Really?' said Arthur, clustering hurriedly round Fenchurch to relieve her of the shopping.

'Yeah,' said Ford, 'at least one of his heads is now saner than an emu on acid.'

'Arthur, who is this?' said Fenchurch.

'Ford Prefect,' said Arthur. 'I may have mentioned him in passing.'

37

For a total of three days and nights the giant silver robot stood in stunned amazement straddling the remains of Knightsbridge, swaying slightly and trying to work out a number of things.

Government deputations came to see it, ranting journalists by the truckload asked each other questions on the air about what they thought of it, flights of fighter bombers tried pathetically to attack it – but no lizards appeared. It scanned the horizon slowly.

At night it was at its most spectacular, floodlit by the teams of television crews who covered it continuously as it continuously did nothing.

It thought and thought and eventually reached a conclusion.

It would have to send out its service robots.

It should have thought of that before, but it was having a number of problems.

The tiny flying robots came screeching out of the hatchway one afternoon in a terrifying cloud of metal. They roamed the surrounding terrain, frantically attacking some things and defending others.

One of them at last found a pet shop with some lizards, but it instantly defended the pet shop for democracy so savagely that little in the area survived.

A turning point came when a crack team of flying screechers discovered the Zoo in Regent's Park, and most particularly the Reptile House.

Learning a little caution from their previous mistakes in the petshop, the flying drills and fretsaws brought some of the larger and fatter iguanas to the giant silver robot, who tried to conduct high-level talks with them.

Eventually the robot announced to the world that despite the full, frank and wide-ranging exchange of views the high-level talks had broken down, the lizards had been retired, and that it, the robot, would take a short holiday somewhere, and for some reason selected Bournemouth.

Ford Prefect, watching it on TV, nodded, laughed, and had another beer.

Immediate preparations were made for its departure.

The flying toolkits screeched and sawed and drilled and fried things with light throughout that day and all through the nighttime, and in the morning, stunningly, a giant mobile gantry started to roll westwards on several roads simultaneously with the robot standing on it, supported within the gantry.

Westward it crawled, like a strange carnival, buzzed around by its servants and helicopters and news coaches, scything through the land until at last it came to Bournemouth, where the robot slowly freed itself of its transport system's embraces and went and lay for ten days on the beach.

It was, of course, by far the most exciting thing that had ever happened to Bournemouth.

Crowds gathered daily along the perimeter which was staked out and guarded as the robot's recreation area, and tried to see what it was doing.

It was doing nothing. It was lying on the beach. It was lying a little awkwardly on its face.

It was a journalist from a local paper who, late one night, managed to do what no one else in the world had so far managed, which was to strike up a brief intelligible conversation with one of the service robots guarding the perimeter.

It was an extraordinary breakthrough.

'I think there's a story in it,' confided the journalist over a cigarette shared through the steel link fence, 'but it needs a good local angle. I've got a little list of questions here,' he went on, rummaging awkwardly in an inner pocket, 'perhaps you could get him, it, whatever you call him, to run through them quickly.'

The little flying ratchet screwdriver said it would see what it could do and screeched off.

A reply was never forthcoming.

Curiously, however, the questions on the piece of paper more or less exactly matched the questions that were going through the massive battle-scarred industrial-quality circuits of the robot's mind. They were these:

'How do you feel about being a robot?'

'How does it feel to be from outer space?' and

'How do you like Bournemouth?'

Early the following day things started to be packed up and within a few days it became apparent that the robot was preparing to leave for good.

'The point is,' said Fenchurch to Ford, 'can you get us on board?'

Ford looked wildly at his watch.

'I have some serious unfinished business to attend to,' he exclaimed.

38

Crowds thronged as close as they could to the giant silver craft, which wasn't very. The immediate perimeter was fenced off and patrolled by the tiny flying service robots. Staked out around that was the army, who had been completely unable to breach that inner perimeter, but were damned if anybody was going to breach them. They in turn were surrounded by a cordon of police, though whether they were there to protect the public from the army or the army from the public, or to guarantee the giant ship's diplomatic immunity and prevent it getting parking tickets was entirely unclear and the subject of much debate.

The inner perimeter fence was now being dismantled. The army stirred uncomfortably, uncertain of how to react to the fact that the reason for their being there seemed as if it was simply going to get up and go.

The giant robot had lurched back aboard the ship at lunchtime, and now it was five o'clock in the afternoon and no further sign had been seen of it. Much had been heard – more grindings and rumblings from deep within the craft, the music of a million hideous malfunctions; but the sense of tense expectation among the crowd was born of the fact that they tensely expected to be disappointed. This wonderful extraordinary thing had come into their lives, and now it was simply going to go without them.

Two people were particularly aware of this sensation. Arthur and Fenchurch scanned the crowd anxiously, unable to find Ford Prefect in it anywhere, or any sign that he had the slightest intention of being there.

'How reliable is he?' asked Fenchurch in a sinking voice.

'How *reliable*?' said Arthur. He gave a hollow laugh. 'How shallow is the ocean?' he said. 'How cold is the sun?'

The last parts of the robot's gantry transport were being carried on board, and the few remaining sections of the perimeter fence were now stacked at the bottom of the ramp waiting to follow them. The soldiers on guard round the ramp bristled meaningfully, orders were barked back and forth, hurried conferences were held, but nothing, of course, could be done about any of it.

Hopelessly, and with no clear plan now, Arthur and Fenchurch pushed forward through the crowd, but since the whole crowd was also trying to push forward through the crowd, this got them nowhere.

And within a few minutes more nothing remained outside the ship, every last link of the fence was aboard. A couple of flying fretsaws and a spirit level seemed to do one last check around the site, and then screamed in through the giant hatchway themselves.

A few seconds passed.

The sounds of mechanical disarray from within changed in intensity, and slowly, heavily, the huge steel ramp began to lift itself back out of the Harrods Food Halls. The sound that accompanied it was the sound of thousands of tense, excited people being completely ignored.

'Hold it!'

A megaphone barked from a taxi which screeched to a halt on the edge of the milling crowd.

'There has been,' barked the megaphone, 'a major scientific break-in! Through. Breakthrough,' it corrected itself. The door flew open and a small man from somewhere in the vicinity of Betelgeuse leapt out wearing a white coat.

'Hold it!' he shouted again, and this time brandished a short squat black rod with lights on it. The lights winked briefly, the ramp paused in its ascent, and then in obedience to the signals from the Thumb (which half the electronic engineers in the galaxy are constantly trying to find fresh ways of jamming, while the other half are constantly trying to find fresh ways of jamming the jamming signals), slowly ground its way downwards again.

Ford Prefect grabbed his megaphone from out of the taxi and started bawling at the crowd through it.

'Make way,' he shouted, 'make way, please, this is a major scientific breakthrough. You and you, get the equipment from the taxi.'

Completely at random he pointed at Arthur and Fenchurch, who wrestled their way back out of the crowd and clustered urgently round the taxi.

'All right, I want you to clear a passage, please, for some important pieces of scientific equipment,' boomed Ford. 'Just everybody keep calm. It's all under control, there's nothing to see. It is merely a major scientific breakthrough. Keep calm now. Important scientific equipment. Clear the way.'

Hungry for new excitement, delighted at this sudden reprieve from disappointment, the crowd enthusiastically fell back and started to open up.

Arthur was a little surprised to see what was printed

on the boxes of important scientific equipment in the back of the taxi.

'Hang your coat over them,' he muttered to Fenchurch as he heaved them out to her. Hurriedly he manoeuvred out the large supermarket trolley that was also jammed against the back seat. It clattered to the ground, and together they loaded the boxes into it.

'Clear a path, please,' shouted Ford again. 'Everything's under proper scientific control.'

'He said you'd pay,' said the taxi-driver to Arthur, who dug out some notes and paid him. There was the distant sound of police sirens.

'Move along there,' shouted Ford, 'and no one will get hurt.'

The crowd surged and closed behind them again, as frantically they pushed and hauled the rattling supermarket trolley through the rubble towards the ramp.

'It's all right,' Ford continued to bellow. 'There's nothing to see, it's all over. None of this is actually happening.'

'Clear the way, please,' boomed a police megaphone from the back of the crowd. 'There's been a break-in, clear the way.'

'Breakthrough,' yelled Ford in competition. 'A scientific breakthrough!'

'This is the police! Clear the way!'

'Scientific equipment! Clear the way!'

'Police! Let us through!'

'Walkmen!' yelled Ford, and pulled half a dozen miniature tape players from his pockets and tossed them into the crowd. The resulting seconds of utter confusion allowed them to get the supermarket trolley to the edge of the ramp, and to haul it up on to the lip of it.

'Hold tight,' muttered Ford, and released a button on

his Electronic Thumb. Beneath them, the huge ramp juddered and began slowly to heave its way upwards.

'OK, kids,' he said as the milling crowd dropped away beneath them and they started to lurch their way along the tilting ramp into the bowels of the ship, 'looks like we're on our way.'

39

Arthur Dent was irritated to be continually wakened by the sound of gunfire.

Being careful not to wake Fenchurch, who was still managing to sleep fitfully, he slid his way out of the maintenance hatchway which they had fashioned into a kind of bunk for themselves, slung himself down the access ladder and prowled the corridors moodily.

They were claustrophobic and ill-lit. The lighting circuits buzzed annoyingly.

That wasn't it, though.

He paused and leaned backwards as a flying power drill flew past him down the dim corridor with a nasty screech, occasionally clanging against the walls like a confused bee as it did so.

That wasn't it either.

He clambered through a bulkhead door and found himself in a larger corridor. Acrid smoke was drifting up from one end so he walked towards the other.

He came to an observation monitor let into the wall behind a plate of toughened but still badly scratched Perspex.

'Would you turn it down, please?' he said to Ford Prefect, who was crouching in front of it in the middle of a pile of bits of video equipment he'd taken from a shop window in Tottenham Court Road, having first hurled a small brick through it, and also a nasty heap of empty beer cans.

'Shhhh!' hissed Ford, and peered with manic concentration at the screen. He was watching *The Magnificent Seven*.

'Just a bit,' said Arthur.

'No!' shouted Ford. 'We're just getting to the good bit! Listen, I finally got it all sorted out, voltage levels, line conversion, everything, and this is the good bit!'

With a sigh and a headache, Arthur sat down beside him and watched the good bit. He listened to Ford's whoops and yells and 'yeeehay!'s as placidly as he could.

'Ford,' he said eventually, when it was all over, and Ford was hunting through a stack of cassettes for the tape of *Casablanca*, 'how come, if . . .'

'This is the big one,' said Ford. 'This is the one I came back for. Do you realize I never saw it all through? Always I missed the end. I saw half of it again the night before the Vogons came. When they blew the place up I thought I'd never get to see it. Hey, what happened with all that, anyway?'

'Just life,' said Arthur, and plucked a beer from a six-pack.

'Oh, that again,' said Ford. 'I thought it might be something like that. I prefer this stuff,' he said as Rick's Bar flickered on to the screen. 'How come if what?'

'What?'

'You started to say, "how come if . . ."'

'How come if you're so rude about the Earth, that you . . . oh never mind, let's just watch the movie.'

'Exactly,' said Ford.

40

There remains little still to tell.

Beyond what used to be known as the Limitless Lightfields of Flanux until the Grey Binding Fiefdoms of Saxaquine were discovered lying behind them, lie the Grey Binding Fiefdoms of Saxaquine.

Within the Grey Binding Fiefdoms of Saxaquine lies the star named Zarss, around which orbits the planet Preliumtarn on which is the land of Sevorbeupstry, and it was to the land of Sevorbeupstry that Arthur and Fenchurch came at last, a little tired by the journey.

And in the land of Sevorbeupstry, they came to the Great Red Plain of Rars, which was bounded on the south side by the Quentulus Quazgar Mountains, on the further side of which, according to the dying words of Prak, they would find in thirty-foot-high letters of fire God's Final Message to His Creation.

According to Prak, if Arthur's memory served him right, the place was guarded by the Lajestic Vantrashell of Lob, and so, after a manner, it proved to be. He was a little man in a strange hat and he sold them a ticket.

'Keep to the left, please,' he said, 'keep to the left,' and hurried on past them on a little scooter.

They realized they were not the first to pass that way, for the path that led around the left of the Great Plain was well worn and dotted with booths. At one they bought a box of fudge, which had been baked in an oven in a cave in the mountain which was heated by the fire of the letters that formed God's Final Message to His Creation. At another they bought some postcards. The letters had been blurred with an airbrush, 'So as not to spoil the Big Surprise!' it said on the reverse.

'Do you know what the message is?' they asked the wizened little lady in the booth.

'Oh yes,' she piped cheerily, 'oh yes!'

She waved them on.

Every twenty miles or so there was a little stone hut with showers and sanitary facilities, but the going was tough, and the high sun baked down on the Great Red Plain, and the Great Red Plain rippled in the heat.

'Is it possible,' asked Arthur at one of the larger booths, 'to rent one of those little scooters? Like the one Lajestic Ventrawhatsit had?'

'The scooters,' said the little lady who was serving at the ice cream bar, 'are not for the devout.'

'Oh well, that's easy, then,' said Fenchurch, 'we're not particularly devout. We're just interested.'

'Then you must turn back now,' said the little lady severely, and when they demurred, sold them a couple of Final Message sunhats and a photograph of themselves with their arms tight around each other on the Great Red Plain of Rars.

They drank a couple of sodas in the shade of the booth and then trudged out into the sun again.

'We're running out of barrier cream,' said Fenchurch after a few more miles. 'We can go to the next booth, or we can return to the previous one which is nearer, but means we have to retrace our steps again.'

They stared ahead at the distant black speck winking in the heat haze; they looked behind themselves. They elected to go on.

They then discovered that they were not only not the first to make this journey, but that they were not the only ones making it now.

Some way ahead of them an awkward low shape was heaving itself wretchedly along the ground, stumbling painfully slowly, half-limping, half-crawling.

It was moving so slowly that before too long they caught the creature up and could see that it was made of worn, scarred and twisted metal.

It groaned at them as they approached it, collapsing in the hot dry dust.

'So much time,' it groaned, 'oh so much time. And pain as well, so much of that, and so much time to suffer it in too. One or the other on its own I could probably manage. It's the two together that really get me down. Oh hello, you again.'

'Marvin?' said Arthur sharply, crouching down beside it. 'Is that you?'

'You were always one,' groaned the aged husk of the robot, 'for the super-intelligent question, weren't you?'

'What is it?' whispered Fenchurch in alarm, crouching behind Arthur, and grasping on to his arm.

'He's sort of an old friend,' said Arthur. 'I . . .'

'Friend!' croaked the robot pathetically. The word died away in a kind of crackle and flakes of rust fell out of his mouth. 'You'll have to excuse me while I try and remember what the word means. My memory banks are not what they were, you know, and any word which falls into disuse for a few zillion years has to get shifted down into auxiliary memory back-up. Ah, here it comes.'

The robot's battered head snapped up a bit as if in thought.

'Hmm,' he said, 'what a curious concept.'

He thought a little longer.

'No,' he said at last, 'don't think I ever came across one of those. Sorry, can't help you there.'

He scraped a knee along pathetically in the dust, and then tried to twist himself up on to his misshapen elbows.

'Is there any last service you would like me to perform for you, perhaps?' he asked in a kind of hollow rattle. 'A piece of paper that perhaps you would like me to pick up for you? Or maybe you would like me,' he continued, 'to open a door?'

His head scratched round in its rusty neck bearings and seemed to scan the distant horizon.

'Don't seem to be any doors around at present,' he said, 'but I'm sure that if we waited long enough, someone would build one. And then,' he said slowly twisting his head around to see Arthur again, 'I could open it for you. I'm quite used to waiting, you know.'

'Arthur,' hissed Fenchurch in his ear sharply, 'you never told me of this. What have you done to this poor creature?'

'Nothing,' insisted Arthur sadly, 'he's always like this . . .'

'Ha!' snapped Marvin. 'Ha!' he repeated. 'What do you know of always? You say "always" to me, who, because of the silly little errands you organic lifeforms keep on sending me through time on, am now thirty-seven times older than the Universe itself? Pick your words with a little more care,' he coughed, 'and tact.'

He rasped his way through a coughing fit and resumed.

'Leave me,' he said, 'go on ahead, leave me to struggle painfully on my way. My time at last is nearly come. My race is nearly run. I fully expect,' he said, feebly waving them on with a broken finger, 'to come in last. It would be fitting. Here I am, brain the size . . .'

Between them they picked him up despite his feeble protests and insults. The metal was so hot it nearly blistered their fingers, but he weighed surprisingly little, and hung limply between their arms.

They carried him with them along the path that ran along the left of the Great Red Plain of Rars towards the encircling mountains of Quentulus Quazgar.

Arthur attempted to explain to Fenchurch, but was too often interrupted by Marvin's dolorous cybernetic ravings.

They tried to see if they could get him some spare parts at one of the booths, and some soothing oil, but Marvin would have none of it.

'I'm all spare parts,' he droned.

'Let me be!' he groaned.

'Every part of me,' he moaned, 'has been replaced at least fifty times . . . except . . .' He seemed almost imperceptibly to brighten for a moment. His head bobbed between them with the effort of memory. 'Do you remember, the first time you ever met me,' he said at last to Arthur, 'I had been given the intellect-stretching task of taking you up to the bridge? I mentioned to you that I had this terrible pain in all the diodes down my left side? That I had asked for them to be replaced but they never were?'

He left a longish pause before he continued. They carried him on between them, under the baking sun that hardly ever seemed to move, let alone set.

'See if you can guess,' said Marvin, when he judged that the pause had become embarrassing enough, 'which parts of me were never replaced? Go on, see if you can guess.

'Ouch,' he added, 'ouch, ouch, ouch, ouch, ouch.'

At last they reached the last of the little booths, set down Marvin between them and rested in the shade. Fenchurch bought some cufflinks for Russell, cufflinks that had set in them little polished pebbles which had been picked up from the Quentulus Quazgar Mountains, directly underneath the letters of fire in which was written God's Final Message to His Creation.

Arthur flipped through a little rack of devotional tracts on the counter, little meditations on the meaning of the Message.

'Ready?' he said to Fenchurch, who nodded.

They heaved up Marvin between them.

They rounded the foot of the Quentulus Quazgar Mountains, and there was the Message written in blazing letters along the crest of the Mountain. There was a little observation vantage point with a rail built along the top of a large rock facing it, from which you could get a good view. It had a little pay-telescope for looking at the letters in detail, but no one would ever use it because the letters burned with the divine brilliance of the heavens and would, if seen through a telescope, have severely damaged the retina and optic nerve.

They gazed at God's Final Message in wonderment, and were slowly and ineffably filled with a great sense of peace, and of final and complete understanding.

Fenchurch sighed. 'Yes,' she said, 'that was it.'

They had been staring at it for fully ten minutes before they became aware that Marvin, hanging between their shoulders, was in difficulties. The robot could no longer lift his head, had not read the message. They lifted his head, but he complained that his vision circuits had almost gone.

They found a coin and helped him to the telescope. He complained and insulted them, but they helped him look at each individual letter in turn. The first letter was a 'w', the second an 'e'. Then there was a gap. An 'a' followed, then a 'p', an 'o' and an 'l'.

Marvin paused for a rest.

After a few moments they resumed and let him see the 'o', the 'g', the 'i', the 's' and the 'e'.

The next two words were 'for' and 'the'. The last one was a long one, and Marvin needed another rest before he could tackle it.

It started with 'i', then 'n' then a 'c'. Next came an 'o' and an 'n', followed by a 'v', an 'e', another 'n' and an 'i'.

After a final pause, Marvin gathered his strength for the last stretch.

He read the 'e', the 'n', the 'c' and at last the final 'e', and staggered back into their arms.

'I think,' he murmured at last, from deep within his corroding rattling thorax, 'I feel good about it.'

The lights went out in his eyes for absolutely the very last time ever.

Luckily, there was a stall nearby where you could rent scooters from guys with green wings.

Epilogue

One of the greatest benefactors of all lifekind was a man who couldn't keep his mind on the job in hand.

Brilliant?

Certainly.

One of the foremost genetic engineers of his or any other generation, including a number he had designed himself?

Without a doubt.

The problem was that he was far too interested in things which he shouldn't be interested in, at least, as people would tell him, not *now*.

He was also, partly because of this, of a rather irritable disposition.

So when his world was threatened by terrible invaders from a distant star, who were still a fair way off but travelling fast, he, Blart Versenwald III (his name was Blart Versenwald III, which is not strictly relevant, but quite interesting because – never mind, that was his name and we can talk about why it's interesting later), was sent into guarded seclusion by the masters of his race with instructions to design a breed of fanatical superwarriors to resist and vanquish the feared invaders, do it quickly and, they told him, 'Concentrate!'

So he sat by a window and looked out at a summer lawn and designed and designed and designed, but inevitably got a little distracted by things, and by the time the invaders were practically in orbit round them, had come up with a remarkable new breed of super-fly that could, unaided, figure out how to fly through the open half of a half-open window, and also an off switch for children. Celebrations of these remarkable achievements seemed doomed to be shortlived because disaster was imminent as the alien ships were landing. But astoundingly, the fearsome invaders who, like most warlike races, were only on the rampage because they couldn't cope with things at home, were stunned by Versenwald's extraordinary breakthroughs, joined in the celebrations and were instantly prevailed upon to sign a wide-ranging series of trading agreements and set up a programme of cultural exchanges. And, in an astonishing reversal of normal practice in the conduct of such matters, everybody concerned lived happily ever after.

There was a point to this story, but it has temporarily escaped the chronicler's mind.